7th Heaven.

RIVALS

by Amanda Christie

Based on the hit TV series
created by Brenda Hampton

And based on the following episodes:
"Let's Talk About Sex"
Written by Brenda Hampton

"Nobody Knows..."
Written by Brenda Hampton & Catherine LePard

Random House 🏠 New York

www.randomhouse.com/kids

Library of Congress Catalog Card Number: 99-068122
ISBN: 0-375-80337-8

Printed in the United States of America
January 2000
10 9 8 7 6 5 4

ONE

"This place is pretty busy for a Thursday afternoon," said Mrs. Camden, resting her hands on her very pregnant tummy.

Mary and Lucy leaned against the family station wagon as they watched the action. They were waiting in front of the Department of Motor Vehicles office, where Mary was about to take her first driver's test.

"Looks like you're next," Lucy observed with a wry smile.

A car horn suddenly blared. Mary jumped, startled by the noise.

"Are you a little nervous, honey?" Mrs. Camden asked.

Mary shook her head. "Not at all," she insisted.

"Well...then I'm going over to that pay phone to check in with your dad," said Mrs. Camden.

Mary and Lucy both smiled.

"I have to remind him about Simon's class!" their mother added hastily.

"Sure, Mom," Lucy nodded, still smiling. "Go on. We'll be right here."

Mrs. Camden walked away.

"Those two should be locked up," Mary said, watching her mother.

"But not together," Lucy added.

Mary smiled. "They can't keep their hands off each other now that Mom's having twins."

The girls paused for a moment and exchanged worried glances.

"You don't think there could be *more* Camdens in our future?" Lucy cried.

Mary frowned, then shivered in mock horror. "Let's just drop it," she insisted. "The whole subject is making me queasy. Besides, I have to figure out what to do if that test guy asks me to parallel park."

"I'm no expert..." Lucy replied, "but I'd do whatever he asks."

"Very inspiring advice," Mary sneered. "Thank you."

Just then, an older man with thick

glasses and a haggard expression walked up to the two girls. He was wearing an official-looking uniform.

"Mary Camden," he said, staring at the clipboard he held in his hand.

"That's me," Mary answered, her heart beginning to race.

"I'll be right with you," the man said over his shoulder as he walked toward the building.

Mary sighed in relief. "If I had a prayer of actually being able to parallel park, I *would* do exactly as he asks," she said. "But as it is..."

"How can you not know how to parallel park a car?" Lucy demanded. "You just finished driver's ed."

"Because my driver's ed. teacher was a moron!" Mary cried. "He couldn't explain it well enough for me, okay?"

"Okay!" Lucy replied, stepping away from her sister. "Don't get all frantic on me. I'm just trying to help."

The girls stood in silence for a moment.

"Then why are we here?" Lucy asked, timidly. "If you can't park, you can't pass."

Mary gave her sister a sidelong glance. Then, she smiled.

"Not true," Mary replied. "I've talked to

some of the kids in my class. They told me the examiner doesn't always ask for parallel parking."

Lucy gave Mary a look of pity. "That's great," she said. "But what do you do if he *does* ask you?"

Mary shrugged. "I'll say I don't know how."

"Really?" Lucy said, surprised. "I'd start crying. In fact, I would cry so hard that the examiner would feel too guilty to fail me."

"That's great," Mary replied. "That's probably the oldest trick in the book. I've never heard of an examiner falling for that one."

"Well, if I were you, I'd try it," Lucy said. "It can't hurt."

"It's not going to matter, because he's not going to ask," said Mary.

Before Lucy could say another word, the examiner returned. "I'm Leon Dougherty," he said, shaking Mary's hand. "Are you ready, Ms. Camden?"

Mary smiled weakly. "All set," she announced as confidently as possible.

Lucy rolled her eyes. "Good luck," she said, stepping away from the car.

Mr. Dougherty gestured to Mary to get behind the wheel. Then he went around the station wagon and climbed into the passenger seat, next to her.

Mary started the car and began to drive away as Lucy watched. With a sudden burst of enthusiasm, Mary waved good-bye to her sister as she drove past.

"Dead girl driving," Lucy whispered to herself, as she watched her sister head for the test track.

Mrs. Camden smiled into the phone.

"How about if I set all the clocks ahead one hour?" she suggested. "That should trick the kids into bed at nine!"

She heard her husband laugh on the other end of the line.

"I think it'll work," Rev. Camden replied. "All we have to do is snatch their watches and change the time on them, too. It's a cinch."

"I'd do anything for an hour alone with you," Mrs. Camden sighed. Then she spotted the station wagon pulling away from the curb.

"Mary's starting her test," Mrs. Camden said. "I'd better get going."

"You didn't tell her that we know she can't parallel park, did you?" Rev. Camden asked.

"No way," Mrs. Camden replied. "She'd hate us if we told her that she wasn't ready for her driver's exam. But if the examiner tells her, well, then she can hate *him* instead."

"Honey, you're a genius."

Mrs. Camden smiled. "I know."

"I'll see you later," said Rev. Camden.

"At the community center!" Mrs. Camden reminded him. "Don't forget about Simon's baby-sitting class."

"It's marked on my desk calendar," Rev. Camden said. "I'll see you there."

Mrs. Camden hung up the phone and walked over to Lucy. "How do you think she'll do?" she asked her daughter.

"No comment," Lucy said with a little grin.

"What's that supposed to mean?" asked Mrs. Camden.

"Dad's sermon from last Sunday," Lucy replied. "If you've got nothing nice to say, just say nothing."

"Good point," said Mrs. Camden.

*　　*　　*

Mary was very careful to signal before she

turned the steering wheel. As she rounded the corner, her eyes never left the road.

"Pull over next to those plastic cones," Mr. Dougherty instructed her.

Mary signaled and stopped the car near two sets of plastic cones.

"How am I doing?" she asked nervously.

"You're doing very well," Mr. Dougherty replied. "You're a very good driver."

Mary smiled brightly as Mr. Dougherty wrote on his clipboard. Then he pointed to the space between the cones. "Now let's see your parallel parking."

Mary's heart froze. She gulped nervously, trying to control her rising panic. She took a deep breath and threw the car into reverse. Then she turned the steering wheel and put her foot on the gas.

The station wagon leapt backward with a lurching motion that threw Mary and Mr. Dougherty against their seat belts. Mary slammed on the brakes. Mr. Dougherty dropped his clipboard and pen.

Determined to finish the task, Mary shifted gears. This time, the car moved forward so fast that it sent the plastic cones flying in all directions.

Mary slammed on the brakes once

again. The station wagon came to a shuddering stop, and the engine stalled out. She turned and looked at Mr. Dougherty. Suddenly, her lower lip began to quiver, and she covered her eyes.

"I'm so sorry!" she blubbered. "It's just that..."

"It's just that...what?" Mr. Dougherty asked, a bit rattled by the ride. "It's just that you don't know how to parallel park?" he asked, a little annoyed.

Mary didn't know what to do. She sat there completely at a loss. Then her sister's advice came to her. *I would start crying so hard that the examiner would feel too guilty to fail me.* Mary burst into mock tears.

"It's just...it's just that there's so much pressure..." Mary began to moan dramatically.

Mr. Dougherty shifted uncomfortably in the passenger seat.

"Young lady," he said, clearing his throat, "you really must get ahold of yourself..."

"There's too much pressure!" Mary cried, deciding to be even more dramatic. "The pressure to be the best at varsity basketball! The pressure to get good grades.

It's all just too much! I can't be good at everything...," Mary quickly swung around and faced the test examiner. "Can I?" she whispered, wiping away false tears.

Her eyes were wide and pleading. Mr. Dougherty fumbled around, looking for his pen and clipboard. Mary sniffed loudly. Mr. Dougherty noticed that her lips were quivering. He looked down at the clipboard in his hand and raised his pen. A moment later, he began to write.

Matt had just pulled a cookie from the jar when Mary and Lucy entered the kitchen through the back door.

"How'd you do?" Matt asked.

"I got it," Mary replied without enthusiasm.

Matt looked at his sister suspiciously. "You got your license?"

Mary halted and faced him. "Yes," she said flatly. "Why are you so surprised?"

Matt gave her a wounded look. "I'm not surprised," he said. "Congratulations, sis."

"Yeah," Mary said, brushing past him. "Thanks a lot."

Mary ran up the steps with Lucy at her heels. Then Mrs. Camden came through the back door. Matt looked at his mother questioningly.

"I'm surprised, too," she told him. "Very surprised."

Mary slammed the bedroom door in Lucy's face. Lucy pulled it open and walked toward her sister.

"You did it, didn't you?" Lucy demanded.

"Did *what?*" Mary replied.

"You took my advice," Lucy continued. "For the very first time, my big sister took my advice."

Mary shrugged. "So what if I did?"

Lucy looked shocked. "You really did take my advice?" she said. "You actually cried?"

"Shhhhh!" Mary said, covering Lucy's mouth with her hand. "I only did it because you told me to..." Mary said, her voice barely above a whisper.

"Well, it worked," Lucy whispered. "So what are you so mad about?"

Mary shook her head. "I shouldn't have to cheat to win," she said. "I'm a disgrace to women drivers everywhere."

"Yeah," Lucy said with a nod. "But not because you cried—because you can't parallel park."

"Don't say another word," Mary demanded.

Lucy rose and walked to the door. She turned and faced her sister.

"Actually, crying to get your way isn't a disgrace to all women drivers," she said. "It's a disgrace to all women. *Period*."

Mary screamed and chased Lucy down the hall.

"I'll get it!" Simon cried when the doorbell rang.

He opened the front door to find Jordan, Lucy's boyfriend, standing on the doorstep.

"Hey, Simon," Jordan said.

"Hey!" Simon replied.

"Is Lucy home?" Jordan asked.

"Yeah," Simon said, turning his head and shouting at the top of his lungs. "*Lucyyyy!*"

Jordan covered his ears. "Thanks," he muttered.

Mrs. Camden came into the foyer. "What's all this yelling about?" she asked. "Oh, hi, Jordan. Come on in," she said. "I've just made some cookies. Lucy will be with you after I have a talk with her."

"But we've got to go, Mom!" Simon said urgently. "We'll be late for my class."

"Okay, okay," Mrs. Camden replied. "Let me speak with Lucy, and then we can go."

Suddenly, Mary came down the steps, and threw a basketball to Jordan. He snatched it out of the air.

"Lucy's busy. She told me to entertain you for a few minutes. Are you ready for some hoops?" she asked.

"If that's what you want to do," Jordan replied.

"That's what I want to do!" Mary said, pushing him out the door.

In the kitchen, Mrs. Camden handed Lucy a list. "Here's where we can be reached," she said. "Ruthie is up in her room playing, so she shouldn't be much trouble."

"Mom!" Lucy cried, gazing at the list. "You're only going to Glenoak Community Center. I think I can take care of Ruthie for an hour or two without an owner's manual. It's not like you're going to the moon or anything."

"You can never be too prepared," Mrs. Camden said.

"Don't worry," Simon informed Lucy. "When I complete my baby-sitting classes, I'll take this job off your hands."

Lucy looked at her little brother in disbelief.

"At a nice price, of course," Simon added.

Mrs. Camden rolled her eyes. "Let's go," she said, pushing Simon out the door, "or we'll be late meeting your father."

"Point!" Mary cried, pushing past Jordan.

Jordan quickly sidestepped the onrushing girl, but he couldn't stop her from making another basket.

Mary dribbled and circled her opponent.

"You better think faster than that, buster," Mary warned before rushing Jordan again. This time, he stood his ground, forcing Mary to change her strategy.

Mary managed to slip past Jordan. But he wouldn't give her any ground, and he moved toward her. Their feet became entangled under the basket. Jordan fell to the floor, but Mary caught her balance and sunk the ball for the second time in less than a minute.

She reached down and helped Jordan to his feet.

"What happened to your legendary defense?" Mary asked.

Jordan dusted himself off. "I guess I don't play to humiliate the other player—or kill them."

"What are you saying—you think I want to humiliate you?" she said, spinning the basketball on her finger.

"Not exactly," Jordan replied. "It's just that you always seem to have to prove something."

Mary smiled devilishly. "Like that I'm better at hoops than you?"

Jordan shook his head. "Like you want everyone to think that you're better than they are."

"That's deep. Very profound. I'll bet you dazzle Lucy with that kind of talk." Mary held out the ball to Jordan. "Two out of three?"

"You're on," Jordan declared.

"Loser has to carry the winner back to the house!" Mary yelled.

Twenty minutes later, Jordan entered the Camdens' kitchen with Mary over his shoulders in a fireman's carry.

"You can put me down now, you big loser," Mary said. Jordan dropped her. Mary filled two glasses with ice water and handed one to Jordan.

"Congratulations on passing your driver's test," Jordan said.

Mary shrugged. She said nothing as Lucy entered the kitchen and kissed Jordan on the cheek.

"Hey, Jordan," Lucy said. "Sorry I can't play this afternoon. I'm on babysitting duty."

"Don't worry about it," Jordan replied, glancing at his watch. "I guess I'd better go anyway. I have to stop by my job and pick up my check." Then Jordan looked at Mary.

"Are you still going tomorrow night?" he asked.

Mary hesitated before answering. When she spoke, she glanced at her sister.

"Yeah," Mary said softly. "I'm going."

Lucy stared at them both, her expression curious.

When Jordan was out the door, Mary tried to slip past Lucy. But her little sister grabbed her.

"Just exactly where were you guys going tomorrow night?" Lucy demanded.

"Nowhere," Mary said, trying to slip

away.

But Lucy still gripped Mary's arm.

"I thought you were going to the girls' basketball sleepover tomorrow night."

Mary pulled away from Lucy and took off up the steps.

"This isn't over," Lucy called after her sister.

Lucy checked on Ruthie, who had fallen asleep. Then she slipped away and headed for her and Mary's bedroom. Mary was there, studying.

"Well?" Lucy demanded.

Mary faced her sister. "Well…what?"

Lucy crossed her arms and glared at Mary.

Mary sighed. "The basketball sleepover tomorrow night, just like the one last Friday night, is…" Mary paused for a moment.

"Is?" Lucy said impatiently.

"Co-ed," Mary finished.

Lucy gasped. "Co-ed?"

"Tina Caldwell's parents are letting us stay in their basement," Mary explained. "We're bringing CDs, videos, food. We're just going to hang out."

"Right," Lucy said, doubtfully.

"We'll do the exact same stuff that we always do at the all-girls sleepovers," Mary continued. "Only the guys' varsity team will be there, too."

Lucy's eyes were wide. "A co-ed sleepover?" she mumbled to herself in disbelief.

"Yes," Mary said. "It's a co-ed sleepover. It's no big deal. I don't see why you should have a problem with it."

Lucy shook her head. "I don't have a problem," she announced. "I'm just surprised Mom and Dad don't have a problem. What did they say?"

Mary squirmed. "Nothing," she muttered after a pause. "They'll probably say something once I tell them, but I haven't yet. And you're not saying anything to them, either. Not if you value living."

Mary rose and left the bedroom. Lucy followed her sister out into the hall.

"Fine!" Lucy barked. "So Jordan's gone to one of these sleepovers?"

Mary nodded. "Just one," she said.

Lucy shook her head doubtfully. "Yeah, right," she said. "Just how dumb do you think I am? I'm not as gullible as Mom and Dad, you know."

Just then, Matt walked down the stairs from his room in the attic. Mary and Lucy immediately stopped talking. An uncomfortable silence filled the air.

Matt pulled the earphones of his Walkman off and stared at his sisters.

"What?" he demanded.

"Nothing," Mary and Lucy replied as one.

Matt smiled knowingly. "Talking about boys, huh?"

"No, we weren't," Mary and Lucy replied together again.

"Yes, you were," Matt declared. "I can see it in your faces."

Mary sneered at her older brother. "Just because you can't find a topic for your Human Sexuality project doesn't mean that everyone is talking about sex behind your back."

Matt shot his sisters a questioning look. "How'd you know about that project?"

"Mom told her about it," Lucy explained. "Then Mary told me."

"Well," Matt said. "If either of you has any suggestions, I'm listening."

Sensing a trap, Mary looked at Lucy warily. Matt caught her look. "Okay," he said. "I don't know what's going on here, but if either of you is thinking about having sex, forget it!" He started to walk away, and

Mary sighed with relief. But Matt paused and leaned into Mary's line of sight.

"That means you, Mary," he said sternly.

Then he put his earphones back on and sauntered down the hall.

Mary sighed again. Then she looked at Lucy.

"Do you have something to add?" Mary asked.

"Remember how devious you said Lauren was for dating two boys at the same time?" Lucy asked.

Mary nodded, not sure where her sister was going with this.

"Well, with this sleepover thing and the way you passed your driver's test, I'm beginning to think that you've got Lauren beat."

Before Mary could reply, Lucy rushed off to check on Ruthie.

"Hey, that isn't fair!" Mary called after her.

But deep down, Mary thought Lucy might be right.

T W O

Simon approached the line of tables set up in the crowded lobby of the community center. The title of each class being offered was written in big block letters on white paper at the head of each table. Simon passed the "Holistic Medicine" table, the "Tennis for Everyone" table, and the "Wonders of Vegetarian Cooking" table without a second glance. He halted in front of the table marked "Baby-sitting for Profit." The volunteer behind the table, a pretty young woman with red hair and freckles, gave Simon the sign-up sheet and took his cash without blinking.

"You'll like this class," she said, handing Simon his change. "You'll learn a lot about babies in the next three weeks."

"Thanks," Simon replied. "I feel that it's never too early to seek higher education—or earn a living." He turned to see his mother rushing up to him.

"Sorry, Simon," Mrs. Camden said, breathless. "This place is so crowded that I had to park in the lot across the street."

"It's okay, Mom," Simon said, showing her his receipt. "I'm ready to go."

They walked upstairs. Mrs. Camden hugged her son once they reached the classroom door.

"Have fun," she said.

"It's *education*, Mom," Simon corrected her. "It's not supposed to be fun."

Simon opened the door and entered the classroom. A dozen other students were already there, waiting for the class to begin. Simon stopped in his tracks and scanned the room.

Wow, he thought, smiling. *Higher education might be fun after all.*

"Sorry I'm late," Rev. Camden said. "There's a real mob out there in the parking lot."

"I know," Mrs. Camden said, kissing his cheek. "Simon's already in class."

"How's he doing?"

Mrs. Camden laughed. "He couldn't be happier—he's the only male in the class!" she said.

Rev. Camden checked his watch. "I have to speak with Carlo Forte before his cooking class begins."

"Next month's bake sale?" Mrs. Camden asked. Rev. Camden nodded and turned down the hall.

Mrs. Camden walked through the community center's halls looking for a phone. She wanted to call Lucy and check up on her.

As she rounded a corner, Mrs. Camden heard sobbing. A teenage girl with long blond hair, obviously pregnant, was leaning against the wall. Tears were rolling down her cheeks. Another girl, about the same age, was trying to comfort her. But she looked like she could use a shoulder to lean on, too.

Mrs. Camden looked beyond the girls to the sign outside the classroom. She frowned. She was about to approach the girls when they suddenly turned and walked into the classroom.

Mrs. Camden paused, taking a deep breath. Then she followed them inside. An attractive woman approached Mrs.

Camden as she entered the room.

"Are you looking for the 'My First Baby' class?" the woman asked.

Mrs. Camden smiled. "Actually, no," she said. "But thanks for the compliment."

The woman smiled, too. "Are you a mother for a second time?"

"Mother of seven," Mrs. Camden replied proudly. "Including twins in a few months."

The teacher chuckled. "You should stay," she said. "You could be our visiting guest speaker."

"I'm Annie Camden," Mrs. Camden said, introducing herself.

"Shelly James," the woman replied, shaking her hand. "I have three kids of my own."

"Actually, I just brought my son here to sign up for baby-sitting class," Mrs. Camden explained. "I was wandering around, and I saw your class."

"That baby-sitting thing is a very good idea," Mrs. James said wryly. "I should have thought of it myself."

"It was *his* idea," Mrs. Camden said. "Simon thinks baby-sitting will make him a fortune in the next few years."

"Don't you love it when they plan

ahead?" Mrs. James said with a chuckle. "My twelve-year-old is already choosing a medical school."

Both women laughed.

"Excuse me. Are we in the right place?" asked a professional-looking couple in their thirties. The woman was very pregnant.

"By the look of your wife, I'd say yes," Mrs. James replied. "But let me see your voucher."

As Mrs. James helped the newcomers, Mrs. Camden scanned the room. The class was filled with teenage girls. Some of them were with friends. Some were with their mothers or other family members. A few girls were with their boyfriends, who appeared to be teenagers as well.

Mrs. Camden frowned.

"Why do I suddenly feel old?" she muttered.

Mrs. James overheard her and sighed. "We may be older," Mrs. James said sadly. "But we're also a whole lot wiser than these girls. You can bet on that."

Mrs. Camden nodded in agreement. Then she saw the two girls she'd seen in the hallway. The blond girl was still crying.

"Would you like to volunteer your services?" Mrs. James asked, touching Mrs. Camden's arm. "Just until your son's class is over, of course."

Mrs. Camden looked at the sobbing girl and her sad-faced friend.

"Yes," she said, taking off her coat. "Yes, I would."

Mary slammed her textbook shut.

"So then what happens?" Lucy asked. "Is it just all talking until the sun comes up?"

Mary threw down her pen. She'd been trying to study for the last half hour. But it was obvious that that wasn't going to happen until Lucy got all the details about the co-ed sleepover.

"No," Mary said, rolling her eyes. "Eventually, most of us fall asleep."

"Where?"

Mary threw up her hands. "Wherever we can find a place to throw our sleeping bags!"

"And no one throws their sleeping bag on top of someone else's?" Lucy said, skeptically.

"No!" Mary cried, lifting her pen again. "That's it, Lucy! Give it a rest, already!"

"Okay, okay." Lucy bit her lip. "But if

you *were* going to do something with some guy, when would that be?"

"Not in high school," Mary stated. "I'm definitely not going to do anything with a boy in high school."

"So when?" Lucy persisted. "In college?"

"I don't know," Mary said with a shrug. "I guess I'll make a college plan when I get to college. I'm still in high school, so I'm sticking to my high school plan for now."

Lucy leaned forward, staring at her sister. "So why isn't your plan to wait until you're married?"

"It'll probably end up being that," Mary said after a pause. "But as plans go, I don't think that will work for me in the end."

Lucy swallowed. "Because?"

"Because right now it's impossible for me to ever think of myself as married," Mary said. "But if I think like that, then I might start thinking that forever is too long to wait—and then I might do something stupid."

"Stupid?" Lucy said. "Like what?"

Mary paused. "Like chucking the whole plan," she said, her voice low. "So I just stick to my short-term plan because short-term plans are more realistic."

Lucy digested her sister's words. She opened her mouth to speak, but Mary was faster. "For example," she said, "if you don't drop this subject, my short-term plan is to scream for help!"

"Really?" Lucy replied. "Because if help comes, it will be Matt—who's downstairs. Then you'll have to explain to him what we were talking about."

The cordless phone at Lucy's side rang. She grabbed it after the first ring.

"Hello, Jordan," Lucy said. "Hold for a second."

Lucy put the phone to her chest and stared at Mary.

"What now?" Mary cried.

"Some privacy, please."

With a sigh of frustration, Mary gathered up her books and headed for the kitchen.

"I'm back," Lucy announced into the phone. "Did you just get home?"

Lucy was surprised to hear from Jordan so early. He'd just left the Camden home half an hour ago.

"Actually," said Jordan, "I never call you right when I get home. If I did, I'd feel like a total wuss. I like to walk around a minute first."

Lucy rolled her eyes. "Anything exciting happen today?"

"Yeah," Jordan replied. "I decided not to go to the basketball sleepover. Do you want to go out somewhere instead? I got paid. I thought we could spend some of the money together."

"That's your college money," Lucy insisted. Secretly, she was relieved by his decision to skip the co-ed sleepover.

"I know," Jordan said. "But I can spend a little of it. We can do something more exciting than Dairy Shack and bowling."

"A burger and bowling sound great to me," Lucy said. "And you know you've got to save your money."

"Okay, okay!" Jordan relented. "You sound like my mother sometimes."

Lucy was stung by her boyfriend's innocent remark. "You think of me as your *mother?*" she said.

Jordan was flustered. "It—it's not that at all!" he stammered. "It's just that I've never had a girlfriend who worried about my future."

"That's because I care about you," Lucy replied. "What kind of girlfriends did you have before me?"

Jordan didn't reply. Lucy took a deep

breath. "Jordan," she said. "Will you answer a question? A *personal* question?"

"Sure," Jordan replied. "I guess so…"

"I'm only going to ask this once, so pay attention."

"Okay."

"And I want the truth," Lucy added.

"I'm always honest with you," Jordan said softly. "You know that."

There was a long pause before Lucy spoke.

"Have you ever had sex?" she said finally.

Now Jordan was really flustered. There was a long pause while he thought over his reply.

Lucy's heart raced. "Come on!" she said. "A simple yes or no is all it takes."

"Yes," he said with an audible sigh. "And that's as much as I want to say about it."

"Class was a snap," Simon said to his parents. "I had my doll fed, burped, and in a fresh diaper before the rest of the class knew which end to powder!" He leaned against the staircase and crossed his arms.

"I know how to take a temperature, tell

if a cut needs stitches," he said smugly. "I even know how to make someone throw up."

Rev. Camden looked horrified. "You can make someone throw up?"

In the living room, Mary looked up from her textbook. "I can believe that!" she cried.

Simon shot his sister a look.

She shrugged. "It's your gift!" she said.

"I can't believe I have to go back three more Thursdays to get certified," Simon said.

"Yeah, you'd think an hour's worth of training would cover everything there is to know about taking care of kids," Rev. Camden said sarcastically.

"Yeah," Simon replied, missing his father's joke. "You'd think."

"At any rate," Mrs. Camden said, "it'll be nice having your help with the twins after they've been born."

"Oh, please," Simon said. "You can't afford me!"

He ran up the stairs, and Rev. Camden turned to his wife.

"Are we paying for this certification or is he?"

"He is," Mrs. Camden replied.

Rev. Camden shook his head sadly. "Heaven help us."

I thought I knew him. I guess I was wrong... Lucy thought sadly. *Very wrong.*

She opened her math textbook and tried to study. But her mind kept returning to her conversation with Jordan.

I should have known, Lucy decided. *He's good-looking, popular, and older than me. Why wouldn't he be...experienced, too?*

She closed her book and began to wonder why she was so bothered.

Is it that Jordan had another girlfriend? A girlfriend he cared enough about to make out with...to do everything with? Or maybe it's that he hasn't tried to do the same thing with me?

Then her thoughts turned to Mary's sleepover. Despite everything that Mary told her, Lucy still wondered if her sister was being honest when she said she was sticking to her plan.

I've always been the one with the plan, Lucy thought. *Mary is the one who always ad-libs her way through life.*

Mary entered the bedroom and dumped her books on her desk. Lucy quickly opened her book again and pretended she was trying to solve a problem.

Mary was surprised to see that her sister's conversation with Jordan had been so short. She sensed from Lucy's body language that things hadn't gone so well.

Well, Mary decided, *it's none of my business. I won't ask.*

She plopped down on her bed and picked up one of Lucy's magazines. She flipped through the pages, but soon lost interest. She dropped the magazine and stared at the ceiling.

How can Lucy read all that dumb stuff about makeup and how to catch the boy of your dreams? thought Mary.

In general, Mary considering exciting reading to be the sports section of their local newspaper. But Lucy had always been different. She read fashion magazines that focused on beauty tips, meeting the right guy, and living happily ever after.

These were things that Mary either didn't care about—like fashion—or that came easily to her—like guys.

Lucy thinks that guys are this magical thing, Mary thought. *But to me, guys are just guys. They can be fun—sometimes even interesting.*

But Lucy's always going for guys who

are older than she is. What's she thinking about with that? wondered Mary, frowning.

Who cares, Mary decided. *Whatever she's thinking about, it's probably pretty stupid, anyway.*

"You should have seen that classroom," Mrs. Camden said as she climbed the stairs.

"If you combined the ages of every girl in that room, it wouldn't equal a baker's dozen."

"Teenage pregnancy is a huge problem," Rev. Camden said. "Kids should not be having kids."

"There were these two girls in particular—"

"Barbara and Cassandra?" Rev. Camden said, recalling their names.

Mrs. Camden nodded. "That's right. The girls I mentioned in the car. They're so sweet and innocent. They have no idea what they've gotten themselves into. And they aren't equipped to deal with it at all."

Rev. Camden looked at his wife with concern. "What can I do to help?"

"How do you know I want you to help?"

Rev. Camden smiled. "Because I think I

know you pretty well by now, Annie Camden."

Mrs. Camden laughed and hugged her husband.

"I've invited Barbara and Cassandra over tomorrow," she explained. "I'm showing them how to cook a vegetarian meal that they can strain into fresh baby food. But don't worry," Mrs. Camden said. "I won't need you for that one."

Rev. Camden smiled again. "Then what *will* I be looking forward to doing?"

"I was wondering if you could talk Cassandra's boyfriend into coming to class with her," she asked.

Rev. Camden shook his head doubtfully.

"He doesn't have to marry her!" Mrs. Camden insisted.

"I know, but—"

"She just wants him there for the birth of the baby," Mrs. Camden continued. "She doesn't have any family."

Rev. Camden thought about it for a moment, then nodded. "I'll give it my best shot," he said.

Mrs. Camden smiled and kissed him.

Rev. Camden blinked and looked at his wife. "I'm not being bribed, am I?" he asked, his voice full of suspicion.

Mrs. Camden shook her head.

"Fresh cookies, and you're *so* glad to see me," teased Rev. Camden.

She pushed him away. "Very funny."

"What else will I be doing besides... well, what is it that I'm supposed to do now?" he asked her.

"Do you remember at the community center, when you went to find the drinking fountain?"

Rev. Camden nodded.

"Well, I kind of told Barbara's boyfriend—that sweet guy with the funny hat—"

Rev. Camden nodded again. "His name is Sam."

"Yes!" Mrs. Camden said. "Sam. I kind of said that you'd be glad to help him find some work."

Rev. Camden thought about it. "Does he have a high school diploma?"

Mrs. Camden shook her head sadly.

"Graduate Equivalency Degree?"

Mrs. Camden continued to shake her head.

"How about a useful skill?"

Mrs. Camden sighed. "Nope."

Rev. Camden looked suddenly hopeful.

"But at least he doesn't have a criminal record, right?"

Mrs. Camden nodded. "Yeah," she said. "He's got one of those. Possession of... something. I didn't get the details."

"A stolen something? A kidnapped something? A drug something?" Rev. Camden demanded.

"Eric!" Mrs. Camden cried. "I just met these people. I didn't want to butt into every single aspect of their lives."

Rev. Camden smiled doubtfully. "Of course not," he muttered. "That's *my* job."

Mrs. Camden nodded. "Right...We're all going to grab dinner at the pool hall... the girls and I."

Rev. Camden nodded. He finally understood. "Because I'll already be at the pool hall with Sam and the other guy."

"They're teenagers," Mrs. Camden explained. "They're not going to want to hang around the house."

Rev. Camden nodded. "Ours don't."

"I knew you'd understand," Mrs. Camden said.

"That because I think you know me pretty well by now," Rev. Camden said.

Simon was getting ready for bed when

Ruthie came into his room clutching two dolls.

"How was your class?" she asked.

Simon smiled smugly. "Well, I don't want to brag—"

"Since when?" Ruthie said.

Simon rolled his eyes. "What can I do for you?" he asked.

Ruthie thrust her dolls into Simon's arms. "Would you mind baby-sitting Amy and Zin-Zin?" she asked. "I need a little time to myself." Ruthie pointed to her rag doll. "Amy is lactose intolerant," she explained. Then she pointed to her monkey doll. "And Zin-Zin is allergic to strawberries. So be very careful with the bedtime snacks."

Simon threw the dolls on the bed and stuck out his palm.

"I'm a professional, you know," he stated. "That means I don't work for free."

Ruthie threw up her hands. "One lousy class and you're already asking for money?" she cried.

But Simon was unmoved. "Two bucks!" he announced. "Per hour. Per kid."

Ruthie made a big show of pulling money out of her pajamas. She handed a bill to Simon.

"Got change for a twenty?" Ruthie asked.

Simon looked at the bill. It was printed with the Monopoly man's face on it.

"This money isn't real," Simon insisted.

Ruthie leaned close to his ear and cupped her hand. "Neither are they," she whispered.

Simon shoved the dolls back into Ruthie's arms. "Good night and get out!" he said.

Ruthie looked stunned. "A check!" she argued. "How about a check? Do you take checks?"

"No!" Simon barked, pointing to the door. Ruthie made a hasty exit. Simon closed the door behind her.

"Try to be a professional in this house..." Simon cried, "and all you get is grief."

THREE

Friday morning came early at the Camden home. Rev. Camden's private phone rang at six A.M. Mrs. Camden rose and fixed breakfast.

At six-thirty, Rev. Camden came out of the shower and began to dress. "I heard the phone but I didn't answer it," she said.

Rev. Camden nodded. "It was Lou," he replied.

"And what did our esteemed deacon want so early this morning?"

Rev. Camden sighed. "Mrs. Dallion lost her husband," he said sadly.

"Oh, no," Mrs. Camden gasped. "Poor Betsy."

"Lou is picking me up any minute," he said. "We're going over to her house to help make arrangements and, hopefully, be of some comfort."

"Can I help?" asked Mrs. Camden.

"Thanks, but we can handle it," Reverend Camden replied. "But I won't be able to drive the kids to school."

"What about Matt?" Mrs. Camden said.

"I caught him going out the door. I think he had an early study session for a test," said the Reverend.

"There's always Mary," Mrs. Camden said hesitantly.

"Mary?" Rev. Camden said, confused. "Exactly how *did* she do on her driving test?" he asked.

"She passed." Mrs. Camden smiled.

Rev. Camden looked surprised. "How'd she do that?"

Mrs. Camden shrugged. "I don't know. But she did."

"Did she have to parallel park?"

"That was the first thing I asked her," said Mrs. Camden. "She said yes."

"But that's impossible," Rev. Camden said. "Her driver's ed. teacher told me that she couldn't do it. In fact, he went so far as to say that we should keep Happy and the kids inside the house if she even wanted to *practice* parallel parking."

Mrs. Camden shrugged.

"So Mary really is a licensed driver?" Rev. Camden said in disbelief. "She's allowed to drive our car without us, *legally?*"

"Yep," said Mrs. Camden.

Rev. Camden was still dumbfounded. "You realize that this is the end of the world as we know it."

"Yeah," Mrs. Camden said, laughing. "I thought I wasn't ready for it either, but watch this."

"Mary! Lucy! Simon! Ruthie!"

A moment later, the kids stumbled downstairs, awake, but still in their pajamas.

"What's up?" Mary asked, rubbing the sleep out of her eyes.

"I thought your first licensed voyage in the station wagon should be a trip to school," Mrs. Camden announced.

Mary and Lucy exchanged a nervous look.

"Congratulations on getting your license," said Rev. Camden. "I just heard."

"Thanks," Mary said without enthusiasm. "But I really don't know—maybe I'm not ready to drive anywhere just yet."

"Don't be silly," Mrs. Camden said. "That's what licenses are—a license to drive anywhere!"

Mary shifted uncomfortably. Simon and Ruthie picked up on her apprehension.

"It's three miles at the most," Mrs. Camden added. "And you've been there a thousand times. You can do it."

"Maybe Dad can—"

Mary was interrupted by a car horn.

"That's Lou," Rev. Camden said, rushing to the door. "I've got to go." He was out the door before Mary could say any more.

"You can do it, Mary," Mrs. Camden said again.

"They do have a huge parking lot..." Lucy said.

Mary shot her sister a look. "What's that supposed to mean?"

Lucy looked down at her feet. "Nothing," she mumbled.

"Okay, okay!" Mary cried. "Fine. I'll drive them to school."

Mrs. Camden threw Mary the car keys. "Thanks, honey. Have a nice day," she said over her shoulder, heading back to the kitchen to prepare breakfast for Ruthie.

*   *   *

"Hey, Matt!" cried Ben. "Wait up, man."

Matt turned and saw Ben running his way. Both boys were carrying video cameras.

"Is that a rental camera from the film department?" Ben asked.

Matt nodded. "Yep, but I don't really know what to do with it, exactly."

Ben looked puzzled. "You don't have a project yet?"

"Am I the only one in class without a Human Sexuality video idea?" Matt asked.

"I think you just might be," Ben replied. "I'm almost done with mine."

"You're kidding," Matt said in disbelief.

Ben shook his head. "Sorry, Camden, I hate to disappoint you. But really, I'm almost done," said Matt's friend.

"What'd you do?"

"I interviewed your parents about your twisted childhood," Ben replied.

"Ha-ha," Matt said. "Not funny."

"Actually," Ben said, "I got a bunch of guys to look straight into the camera and give their best make out lines."

"Some assignment," said Matt.

"This weekend, I'm going to have women respond to the lines," Ben said. "It could get interesting because some of the lines are funny and some are sensitive, but a lot of them are just plain rude."

"That sounds great," Matt said.

"Then my sister is going to do a monologue where she says that men don't talk women into anything because women have minds of their own." Ben smiled proudly.

"I wish I could think of something half that interesting," said Matt.

"Thanks," Ben replied. Then he patted Matt on the back. "Gotta go to class," he said. "Good luck with your project, pal."

Matt shook his head and crossed the campus green. He had an economics test this morning, so he didn't have time to dwell on his project

Lucy and Simon climbed into the station wagon, engaged in the usual argument over who would sit in the front seat. Except now that Mary was driving, they were arguing over who would sit in the *back*.

"Let's flip a coin," Simon suggested.

"Fine," Lucy cried. "Heads."

Their coin came up tails. Lucy nervously climbed into the front seat next to Mary.

"Belt up," Simon said to Lucy. "You're sitting in what auto insurance companies like to call the 'death seat.' More fatalities occur in that seat than in any other."

Lucy looked out the windshield, then at Mary.

"Don't say a word," Mary said. "You'll be just fine."

Lucy swallowed hard and tried to fasten her seat belt. She was fumbling with the buckle, unable to latch it.

"Hurry up," Mary said. "There won't be anyplace to park."

"You can always park on the street," Simon said. Mary turned around and gave him a cold stare.

"Or...maybe not," he said, confused.

Mary quickly started the engine. Lucy fought the urge to cover her eyes.

I've never made out with a guy, and now I'm going to die, thought Lucy. *Life is a cruel joke.*

At the back door, Mrs. Camden and Ruthie watched Mary drive off.

"Do you think they'll make it, Mom?" Ruthie asked.

Mrs. Camden laughed. "Of course they will," she replied. "Now get ready for school, or you'll miss the bus."

Mrs. Camden watched the station

wagon disappear as Ruthie ran upstairs.

"Of course they will," she whispered to herself.

Despite Lucy's worst fears, she arrived at Walter Reed High School safely. She said good-bye to Mary and quickly disappeared.

Later that morning, between classes, Mary spotted Lucy with Jordan in the hall. Mary leaned against her locker and watched them together. She realized that she hardly knew Jordan, even though she'd talked with him so many times.

Mary had to admit that Jordan was handsome. But she instantly felt guilty for checking out her sister's boyfriend like that.

As she continued to watch her sister with her new boyfriend, Mary noticed that Lucy was getting agitated over something.

As Mary was only a few feet away, she couldn't help but overhear most of their conversation.

"Just tell me *when*," Lucy pleaded. "Or better still, just tell me *who*. Was it someone at this school?"

Jordan tossed his hair, clearly uncomfortable with the conversation.

"Wait a second," Lucy cried suddenly. "Was there more than the one 'who'?"

Jordan rolled his eyes. "Oh, yeah!" he declared. "There was an entire who-ville. Actually, I had an entire who-harem."

"Is that where you went to school before you transferred here?" Lucy asked, trying to make a joke.

"No!" Jordan cried, clearly not finding it funny.

"How about you just stop asking me questions?" Jordan said. "You're making me really sorry that I told you the truth in the first place."

"But—"

"Let's just say that we're done with this subject?" Jordan interrupted.

Lucy tossed her head. She paused for a moment and then strode off without saying a word. A minute later, Mary caught up with her sister.

"I saw your confrontation," Mary said.

Lucy looked stunned.

"I think the whole school heard it, in fact," Mary joked.

"It's driving me crazy," Lucy said. "I've got to know…"

"I think you should give it a rest," Mary said. "I don't know Jordan very well, but I could see him breaking it off with you if you persist."

"What?" Lucy cried, her hands on her hips. "And start dating you?"

Mary was surprised. "What do you mean?"

Lucy paused and then looked at the ground. "Sorry," she grumbled. "I'm just upset."

She leaned against the lockers beside Mary. They both watched as Jordan started talking to a pretty senior girl. Lucy sighed.

"I'm surprised he even asked me out in the first place," Lucy said.

"Why do you say that?" said Mary.

"Every time he kisses me, I bet he's probably thinking about how I'm doing it wrong."

Mary looked at her sister but couldn't think of anything to say.

"He's obviously much more experienced than I realized," Lucy continued.

"So?" Mary said.

"So I can't help but wonder why he's even going out with me and why he hasn't even *tried* anything with me."

Mary smiled. "Maybe because Jordan really cares for you and respects you?" she offered.

Lucy shrugged. "Yeah, and maybe he

just finds me safe and unattractive," she replied sadly.

"Hey, Lucy?" Mary said.

"Yeah?"

"How's the weather in the land of Big-Time Stupid?" Mary said.

Lucy ignored her sister, remaining fixed on Jordan and the girl he was talking to. Lucy noticed the girl reach out and touch his arm. Jordan laughed loudly at a remark she made.

"Maybe I should see if he's really attracted to me," Lucy said thoughtfully.

"What?" Mary said.

Lucy didn't look at her. "You heard me," she said evenly.

"Yeah, I heard you," Mary said. "But are you talking about what I think you're talking about?"

Lucy shrugged, staring at Jordan.

"Forget it," Mary said, starting to laugh.

"What's so funny?" Lucy demanded. "Why *shouldn't* I find out if Jordan is attracted to me? Don't you wonder if guys are really attracted to you?"

"Let's just leave me out of this," Mary replied. "There are plenty of reasons not to find out if Jordan is attracted to you."

"For one?"

Mary raised a finger. "For *one*, this is your second boyfriend after Jimmy Moon." Mary raised a second finger. "Two. You just started dating Jordan. And three, you're still a baby."

"A baby!"

"Yes, a baby," Mary repeated. "And a baby isn't ready for making out yet." Mary stared at her sister a moment and then walked away. Lucy was left fuming.

"I'll show you," Lucy whispered. "I'll find out how Jordan feels about me no matter what you think, big sister..."

After school was done, Mary, Lucy, and Simon walked through the back door of their home. Lucy brushed past both of them and ran upstairs. Simon ran to the cookie jar and grabbed a snack.

"Here're your keys," Mary said, thrusting the car keys into her mother's hand.

"You look pretty glum," Mrs. Camden said. "Aren't you the least bit excited about getting to drive?"

Mary frowned. "Not really," she said with a shrug. "I don't see what the big deal is, anyway."

"I think the big deal is that you've been

looking forward to it for six months," Rev. Camden said as he walked through the back door.

"Well, it's no big deal now, okay?" Mary said.

"Why not, honey?" Mrs. Camden asked.

"It just isn't, okay?" Mary said, beginning to look upset. Mrs. Camden backed off. "Okay," she said softly.

Mary covered her eyes and hurried out of the kitchen. Rev. and Mrs. Camden watched her go, stunned.

Rev. Camden cleared his throat. "Was she...?"

"Crying," Mrs. Camden finished.

"Fake crying?"

"Oh, yeah," Mrs. Camden replied. "As fake as they come. She'll get no Oscars for that performance."

"I wonder..." Rev. Camden said suspiciously.

"So do I," Mrs. Camden nodded. "So do I..."

Mary burst into the bedroom, startling Lucy, who was modeling a new, much shorter skirt.

"Are you crying?" Lucy asked.

"No," Mary replied, wiping her face. "I'm not."

"You sure look like you are," Lucy said.

Mary faced her sister. "Well, I'd hate to tell you what you look like in that short skirt!"

Lucy glanced into the mirror self-consciously. Then she faced her sister again. "So what are you trying to get out of it now?"

"Get out of what?" Mary asked.

"This whole sobbing thing."

Mary sighed. "Mom and Dad started interrogating me about driving," she explained. "So I broke down."

"Just like that?" Lucy said. "Intentionally?"

"Yes," Mary said.

"I can't believe you," Lucy said. "You know that when I cry, I'm actually *really* crying."

Mary faced her. "And yet, strangely enough, it has the same results."

Lucy nodded. "Still," she countered, "at least I'm not faking."

Mary raised her fist. "Would you like me to make you cry for real?"

Lucy faced the mirror again. "No. But thanks anyway," she said sarcastically. "Maybe some other time."

Lucy watched in the mirror as her sister wiped away the rest of her tears. "I've created a monster," Lucy muttered.

Matt came through the back door and set a video camera on the kitchen table.

"Switching your major to film studies?" Mrs. Camden asked.

Matt shook his head. "No, it's for my Human Sexuality class," he explained. "I'm supposed to make some kind of presentation on sex."

"Sounds...interesting," Mrs. Camden said diplomatically.

"Relax, Mom," Matt said, smiling. "I'm just supposed to interview people or something. Nothing too crazy."

"Well, before you film your first documentary, would you mind running to the market for me?" Mrs. Camden asked, handing Matt a list.

"But I just got home," Matt complained. "Can't Dad go?"

"He has a church emergency," Mrs. Camden said. "And he's going to be counseling some troubled teens later on."

"Mary and Lucy?" Matt asked.

"Stop it. That's not funny," Mrs. Camden said, laughing anyway.

"But for real, Mom," Matt continued. "Why can't Mary go to the store? She has a license."

Matt's and his mother's eyes met. They both nodded. "Because Mary can't parallel park," they said in unison.

"There's nothing here but vegetables," Matt said, looking at the list.

"Don't question my grocery list," Mrs. Camden said. "Just get the stuff. Here's some money…and I expect to see some change!"

"Sure, Mom," Matt replied. "Will we be grazing dinner when I get home?"

"Ha-ha. Very funny," Mrs. Camden said, pushing Matt out the back door.

Lucy closed her textbook and cleared her throat.

"What now?" Mary asked, irritated.

"Can I just make one teeny suggestion?" Lucy asked.

"Haven't you already made enough suggestions for one week?" replied Mary.

"I think you should learn how to parallel park and then re-take the test," Lucy said.

Mary turned and leaned toward Lucy. "Why?" she asked. "Because you gave me really bad advice?"

"Well, yes," Lucy said. "And because *you* made a bad decision to follow my bad advice. Of course," Lucy added, "I didn't know you weren't going to cry for real."

"Real, fake," Mary said. "What's the difference? The result is usually the same."

"But when I said cry, I meant just that," Lucy insisted. "Fake crying is like a lie. And you should break the habit now before it controls you."

Mary blinked. *I can't believe my little sister is actually talking...sense.*

"Oh, I'm going to break something, all right," Mary said. "But it's not going to be any habits!" She lunged at Lucy. Both girls went down onto Lucy's bed. They were struggling so hard that they hit the floor with a loud thump.

Suddenly, the door was flung open and Mrs. Camden stood on the threshold with her arms crossed, staring at her daughters. Mary and Lucy jumped to their feet and tried to act casual.

They failed miserably.

Mrs. Camden continued to stare.

"Does anyone want to tell me what's going on?" she demanded.

At that, Mary started to cry.

FOUR

"I don't know what's wrong with me," Mary sobbed, covering her dry eyes with her hands, desperately trying to create tears. When she realized that no tears were coming, she decided to hide the fact by sobbing even louder.

Mrs. Camden went to Mary and hugged her. She looked at Lucy over Mary's shoulder as she patted her oldest daughter on the back. Lucy shrugged and turned away, refusing to meet her mother's gaze.

"Do you want to talk about it, Mary?" Mrs. Camden asked. Mary shook her head and buried her face deeper into her mother's shoulder.

"I guess it's just all the excitement this week," she sniffed. "It's kind of scary, getting my license and all—driving is a major responsibility."

"Yes, it is," Mrs. Camden cooed. "It's a lot to deal with. You must be exhausted."

Mary nodded. She pulled away from her mother, but her hands still covered her face.

"Maybe you should take a nap," Mrs. Camden suggested.

"But, Mom," Mary whined, rubbing her eyes theatrically. "It's only six o'clock."

"I know. But sleep can heal a lot of wounds."

"But I have my basketball sleepover tonight," Mary said.

"Well, all the more reason to take a nap now, so you'll be refreshed for later."

Mrs. Camden looked at Lucy.

"Come on," she said. "Let's leave Mary alone for a while."

"But, Mom," Lucy protested. "I have to study and then get ready for my date with Jordan!"

"You'll have plenty of time for both," Mrs. Camden said. "Come on."

Lucy shrugged. "Let me just get my books," she said as Mrs. Camden left the room. Lucy looked at Mary while she gathered her stuff.

"Don't say a word," Mary warned.

Lucy opened her mouth but said nothing. She grabbed her books, her sewing kit, and her black skirt and hurried off.

Matt came through the back door with grocery bags in hand. He placed them on the kitchen counter.

"No change," he announced. "Carrots and green beans were both on sale, so I bought double the amount—it pays to stock up."

Mrs. Camden smiled. "If only your father thought that far ahead when he shopped."

"Well, if I can't come up with a project for Human Sexuality class, I'll be a grocery store clerk, not a college grad."

"Oh, I don't think that will happen," Mrs. Camden said.

Matt stared off into space and then turned to his mother. "I need inspiration," he whispered.

"Try these," she said.

She presented him with a plate of freshly baked cookies and a glass of milk.

"Thanks, Mom," Matt said. "I gotta go—and I'm not taking any calls."

"Yes, Mr. Camden," she replied with a mock salute. "I'll hold all calls."

Mrs. Camden had just finished putting the veggies into the crisper when Ruthie and Simon entered the kitchen. She watched out of the corner of her eye as they reached into the cookie jar and took the last two cookies.

"What happened to the rest of the cookies?" Simon asked. "I smelled fresh cookies baking half an hour ago."

"I'm saving the rest," Mrs. Camden replied. "I have friends coming over soon."

Ruthie cocked her head. "And we're not your friends?"

Mrs. Camden's heart melted. She walked over to the microwave and withdrew a plate of warm cookies.

"One more," she said, offering them the plate. "But that's it."

While they munched, Mrs. Camden poured some milk.

"So what's on your agenda tonight?" she asked Simon.

He thought for a moment. "You and Dad are going out with your friends later, right?"

Mrs. Camden nodded.

"Well, I was hoping to try out my baby-sitting expertise," Simon said. "But I can't find anyone to baby-sit," he said looking at his little sister.

"I see," said Mrs. Camden.

"Deena tried to help me," Simon said. "But no one will hire me because I don't have experience. But I can't get any experience unless someone hires me."

"It's a fishy circle," Ruthie said.

Mrs. Camden laughed. "I think you mean vicious. It's a *vicious* circle," she said.

"And it should stay that way," Ruthie said, turning to Simon. "Don't look at me — that's just the way these things work!"

Simon continued to stare.

"I mean it!" Ruthie cried. "I can't help you with your baby-sitting experience."

Mrs. Camden took Ruthie's hand. "Actually, honey, Mary's going to a sleep-over," she said. "Lucy has a date with Jordan. And Matt is busy working on his project."

"But I don't want to be Simon's finny pig!" Ruthie said.

"What?" Mrs. Camden asked.

"I think she means *guinea* pig, Mom,"

Simon explained. "Ruthie has fish on her mind."

"Oh." Mrs. Camden blinked. She turned her attention back to Ruthie. "It's just that your dad and I would really enjoy going out tonight."

Ruthie crossed her arms. "I'd like to go out, too."

Mrs. Camden looked at her daughter and smiled. Then she shrugged as if to say she was sorry.

"Mommy!" Ruthie said, her arms flung wide. "Don't make me do it. Don't make me give Simon baby-sitting lessons. Please!"

"Don't worry," Mrs. Camden said. "If you *really* don't want to stay home with Simon, then you don't have to."

"Thanks," Ruthie said, grabbing another cookie. "I definitely don't want to." With that, she ran upstairs.

"Great," Simon said, his shoulders sagging. "There goes my only hope."

"It's not over yet," Mrs. Camden said.

"How's that?"

"Make her *want* to stay home with you," Mrs. Camden said. "Think of it as a lesson in child psychology."

"How do I do that?"

"Convince Ruthie that if she stays home with you, she'll have so much fun that it'll be the time of her life," said Mrs. Camden.

"Fun..." Simon said, becoming suddenly inspired. "The time of her life..."

He nodded, confident that the plan would work. "Okay. Everyone says I'm a fun guy. I can do fun."

Simon raced upstairs.

Mrs. Camden smiled as she watched him go. *I hope he knows what he's getting into,* she thought, taking two cookies off the plate and putting them in the jar. She hid the rest of them in the microwave again.

Simon knocked on Ruthie's door. "Can I come in?" he asked.

"Sure," Ruthie replied. "But you're not making baby-sitting sound like any fun— no matter what you say."

Simon frowned. "You heard Mom."

Ruthie nodded. "I'm not stupid," she said. "I've gone through this baby-sitting thing with Matt, Mary, *and* Lucy."

"Yeah," Simon said. "But did Matt, Mary, or Lucy ever make your bed into a limousine and get Happy to drive you and your dolls to the moon?"

"All three of them," Ruthie replied. "What else have you got, Mr. Fun Guy?"

Simon paused, deep in thought.

"You can't just shuffle me off to the moon and call it baby-sitting," Ruthie said.

"Okay," Simon said. "Let's cut the kid stuff."

"Now you're talking," Ruthie said.

"I'll split whatever I get for baby-sitting you fifty-fifty."

Ruthie's eyes went wide.

"Do you really think Mom and Dad are going to pay you?" she said, laughing.

Maybe she has a point, he thought. *There hasn't been any discussion of money.*

"There's only one way I'll let you baby-sit me," Ruthie said. "You have to let me do whatever I want, whenever I want."

Simon mulled over her proposition briefly. "But no playing with fire or sharp objects," he added.

"Done," Ruthie nodded.

They shook on it, and Simon sauntered out Ruthie's door certain that he'd gotten the best of the deal. But if he had heard Ruthie's laughter, he might have realized his troubles were only beginning.

*   *   *

Matt was unlocking his Camaro when Ellen and Janet—two of the prettiest girls from his Human Sexuality class—called out his name. They walked toward him with big smiles on their faces. He dumped his books in the back seat, closed the car door, and walked up to them.

"Hey, Matt," Janet said. "Want to grab some pizza?"

Matt smiled. "I'd love to, but I really have—"

"Oh, come on, Matt," Ellen insisted. "Have a little fun." She tilted her head and ran her hands through her long brown hair as she talked.

"Believe me, I'd really like to," Matt said. "But I'm way behind on my project."

"I understand," Janet replied. "I wouldn't be going out if I hadn't already handed in my project."

Matt was stunned. "You're kidding!" he cried.

"Mine's in, too," Ellen said.

"What was your project on?" Matt asked her.

"I interviewed female athletes as a part of a study on why women in sports are less likely to become pregnant before they're married," she said, smiling proudly.

"Wow," Matt said. "That's actually good to hear—my younger sister plays basketball in high school."

Then Matt faced Janet. "And what'd you do?"

"I used my grandparents," Janet said.

"Huh?"

She nodded enthusiastically. "I talked to them and some other couples who have been married for fifty years or more and are still madly in love."

Matt nodded, impressed. "That's a great subject, too."

"How about you, Matt?" Janet asked.

"Me," Matt shrugged. "I've got nothing. I'm blocked. My mind's a total blank."

Ellen rolled her eyes. Janet shook her head in disbelief. "You can't think of a single subject about sex?" asked Ellen.

"That's hard to believe," Janet added.

"Why's that?" said Matt.

The girls exchanged meaningful looks. "Oh, I don't know," Janet said, refusing to meet his eyes. But the tone of her voice gave her away.

Ellen smiled slyly. "It's just that you *look* like you think about sex all the time," she said.

Matt blinked, unsure of what she

meant. Then he decided that maybe he didn't want to know after all. So he remained silent.

"Well, I guess we'll see you Monday," Janet said.

"Yeah, have a good weekend, Matt," Ellen said with a toss of her head.

Matt leaned against his Camaro deep in thought as they walked off.

If I really look like I think about sex all the time, then why can't I come up with a project?

Lucy was walking back to her and Mary's room to study a bit before getting ready for her date with Jordan. She decided that it was still too early to get dressed for their big night. *At least studying is better than helping Mom prepare the vegetarian baby food,* she decided.

Lucy pushed the bedroom door open with her foot. Her arms were filled with books. A brown paper bag was perched on top of them. As she entered the room, Lucy discovered that Mary had awakened from her nap and was busy gathering her stuff for the sleepover. Lucy dropped her books on her desk and thrust the brown paper bag under Mary's nose.

"Mom told me to give you these cookies for the sleepover."

Mary took the bag and tossed it on top of her sleeping bag without saying thanks. Lucy stared at her.

"Not a word to anyone," Mary said. "I'm not doing anything wrong."

"I won't say a thing," Lucy replied. "If you want to go to a co-ed sleepover, that's your personal business."

"Fine!" Mary said. She went to the closet and started pulling out clothes.

"But I *do* wonder if Mom would've given you those cookies if she knew the sleepover was going to be co-ed..." Lucy said.

The cordless phone rang before Mary could respond. She quickly grabbed it. "Hello?" Mary said, a twinge of anger in her voice. She listened for a moment, then thrust the phone into Lucy's hand.

"It's Jordan."

Mary gathered up a bundle of clothes. Then she snatched up her knapsack and flew out the door, slamming it behind her.

Lucy took a deep breath. "Hi," she said. "Jordan, before you say anything, I want to apologize for giving you the third degree today."

She felt better once she heard him laughing. "That's okay," he said. "I've been thinking that maybe we *should* talk about it."

"That's okay," Lucy replied. "I was just being immature. I don't have to know *everything* about you."

"But maybe I want to tell you," said Jordan.

"But what if there're things about me I don't want you to know," Lucy teased.

"All right, you win," Jordan said, laughing again. "Where do you want to go tonight? A bunch of my friends are going to the bowling alley before they crash that sleepover."

Mention of the sleepover bothered Lucy. "You've never gone to more than one of those sleepovers, have you?" she asked.

"Nope," Jordan replied without hesitation. "I decided not to attend after the first one. I felt kind of funny about the whole thing."

Lucy's couldn't help but sigh with relief.

"So, is it bowling?" Jordan asked.

"I don't really feel like hanging out with a group tonight," Lucy said. "Is there someplace we can go to be alone?"

"Like your living room?" Jordan said.

"No," Lucy replied. "Someplace where we won't be interrupted. Maybe we can just go for a drive and talk."

Jordan was quiet for a moment. "I don't know what's going on here," he said finally. "But you and I both know that your parents prefer we hang out with a group."

"So?" Lucy said, a little irritated. Jordan's response was not what she had been hoping to hear.

"I can't imagine asking your dad—the Reverend—if it's okay to take a moonlit drive to nowhere with his daughter," Jordan said.

"So don't ask," Lucy said in a soft whisper.

"What?" Jordan said. "Why are you whispering?"

Lucy rolled her eyes.

"Just pick me up at eight," she said, hanging up the phone. Then she bunched her hands into fists and pounded her bed until her arms were tired.

Mary entered the room just in time to see the end of her sister's outburst.

"So!" Mary said in a loud voice that made Lucy jump. "What did you and Jordan decide to do tonight?"

Lucy stood up with her chin raised

high, hoping to regain her dignity. "That would be none of your business," she declared.

Just then, loud music began to blast from downstairs. Mary and Lucy dropped the subject and darted into the hallway. The music became even louder. It was coming from the kitchen.

"Is Mom having a party?" Lucy asked.

Mary shrugged and the girls rushed downstairs.

Am I truly clueless? Matt wondered as he drove home from his classes. *Why else would I be the only person in class who doesn't have a project yet?*

And it's due Monday.

A car swerved into his lane, forcing Matt to react quickly to avoid an accident. His frustration turned to anger. But he resisted the urge to pound the steering wheel or yell at the other driver.

If I lose it now, I'll never come up with a project. And then I'll flunk, get thrown out of college, and work at the Dairy Shack flipping burgers for the rest of my life—all because I'm totally clueless!

Matt ran his hand through his hair as the dire consequences played in his mind.

Maybe I'm thinking about this too hard, he decided. *Maybe I should go home and lighten up. Listen to a little music, and inspiration will just come to me.*

Wouldn't that be nice?

FIVE

"You both need to try to remain positive," Mrs. Camden said. She dropped the vegetable strainer into the sink.

"It's hard, Mrs. Camden," Cassandra said.

"Yeah," Barbara added. "Having a baby is tough enough. But it's even tougher when you have to go through it alone."

Mrs. Camden turned and faced the two teenage girls, who were sitting at the Camdens' kitchen table, peeling and cleaning vegetables. "Have you both been following your diets?" she asked.

The girls nodded. "That's the easy part," Barbara explained. "It's the exercise that gets to me."

"Yeah," Cassandra said. "I can hardly get out of a chair, let alone walk around the block."

"The constant backache," Barbara said.

"The morning sickness," Cassandra added.

"And the kicking," they said in unison.

"Well," Mrs. Camden said, nodding wisely. "I think I know a way to remain positive and get your exercise at the same time."

The girls looked at her expectantly.

"I have a little tape right here," she said, flipping the switch on a tape recorder. Music blasted from the speakers and filled the kitchen. Mrs. Camden pumped up the volume. Then she turned and faced the girls.

"It's called the 'Locomotion,'" Mrs. Camden cried over the music. "And it goes like this…"

She began to dance around the room, teaching the girls the step. The teenagers hopped to their feet and got into the music. Soon, the three of them were laughing and dancing in a conga line around the table. Happy ran into the kitchen, barked, and joined the fun. She ran in circles, jumping around to the beat.

Cassandra grabbed a wooden spoon from the stove and used it as a microphone. Mrs. Camden and Barbara watched as she sang and danced. Soon Barbara and Mrs. Camden were rocking behind her, doing backup vocals.

Out of the corner of her eye, Mrs. Camden noticed Mary and Lucy were watching them from the doorway. She danced over to her daughters and tried to pull them into the fun. But neither Mary nor Lucy would budge.

Cassandra reached for the recorder and shut it off. Mrs. Camden stepped back and made hasty introductions. "Barbara, Cassandra, these are two of my babies," Mrs. Camden said. "Mary and Lucy."

Her daughters both smiled weakly. Then their eyes strayed to their guests' bellies. "Mary is sixteen, and I'm fifteen," Lucy announced.

Barbara smiled. "I'm sixteen, too," she said.

Cassandra raised her hand. "Me too," she said. "But I'm almost seventeen."

Mary nodded and smiled. Inside, she was horrified that these two mothers-to-be were the exact same age as she. But she hid her feelings and shook hands with both of them, trying to be as polite as possible. Lucy did the same.

Mrs. Camden noticed Mary's discomfort and smiled inwardly.

This is better than any lecture Eric or I could have given her, she thought happily. *Thank goodness I don't have to worry about Lucy yet.*

"Are you having a baby shower?" Mary asked.

"Yeah," Lucy said. "I thought there was a party going on."

Barbara and Cassandra laughed.

"I'm giving the girls a little cooking lesson," Mrs. Camden explained. "We expecting mothers have to eat right. Want to join us?"

"That's okay," Mary said. "I'm on my way to the sleepover."

"And I'm going out with Jordan," Lucy chimed in. "We'll probably grab a burger at the Dairy Shack or something."

Cassandra looked hard at Lucy. "Be careful," she said. "Seven months ago I went out for a burger, and look at me now."

"I went out for sushi," Barbara added. "I thought I was being sophisticated."

A look of horror crossed Mary's and Lucy's faces. Barbara and Cassandra laughed.

Mrs. Camden looked at Lucy. "Are you and Jordan meeting friends?" she asked.

Lucy shrugged. "We usually do," she replied.

"Yes," Mrs. Camden said. "You *usually* do, but what about tonight? Where will you and Jordan and your friends be meeting?"

"I don't know," Lucy said. "I haven't thought about it yet."

"Well *think* about it," Mrs. Camden insisted. "Or call Jordan and find out for me. Okay?"

Lucy looked at Mary. Mrs. Camden looked at Mary and then back at Lucy. She was beginning to get the feeling that something was up.

"I know where your sister is going to be," Mrs. Camden said. "And I want to know where you and your date are going to be."

Lucy said nothing.

"I didn't know it was going to be such a challenging question," Mrs. Camden said.

"Okay, okay," Lucy sighed. "I'll think about it right away."

Mary realized that she had to get out of there in a hurry or her cover would be blown. "It was really nice meeting you guys," she said.

"Yeah," Lucy added.

The sisters scurried out of the kitchen as quickly as they could.

"Ohhh," Cassandra said, clutching her stomach. "This one is still dancing."

She placed Mrs. Camden's hand on her belly.

"Isn't that neat?" Cassandra said.

"Yes," Mrs. Camden sighed. Her own twins were kicking up a fuss.

Cassandra's face suddenly grew serious. "Now if I could just keep her in there until I grow up, finish school, and get a job..." she said sadly.

Mrs. Camden reached out and gave Cassandra a big hug.

"Doing all those things won't be easy with a baby," she said. "But if you make up your mind that that's what you want, you'll succeed."

Cassandra nodded, tears beginning to well in her eyes.

"Don't worry," Mrs. Camden said. "I'll help you."

"What I really want," said Barbara, "is

to back up seven months and say, 'I don't have anything to prove to you, so back off.'" She laughed. But there was a note of bitterness in her tone, and she suddenly got embarrassed and teary-eyed. Mrs. Camden pulled her close, too.

"I promise to do what I can to help both of you," she said. "You won't have to go through this alone."

At the local pool hall, Rev. Camden was doing his part to help Barbara and Cassandra. He sat at a table with a teenager named Sam, who was Barbara's boyfriend and the father of her baby.

While they talked, Sam was trying to fill out an employment application for a job as a busboy. He looked down at the paper and the many blank spaces, nervously shifting the pen in his hand.

"I've got to fill out all this information just to bus tables?" Sam asked.

Rev. Camden smiled. "It's a formality," he explained. "The manager is definitely going to give you a shot at the job. He told me so."

"Are you sure?" Sam asked doubtfully. "'Cause I don't want to write all this personal stuff down if I'm not getting the job."

He ran his hands through his close-cropped hair and gazed down at the paper as if it were a poisonous snake.

"They know...your background," Rev. Camden said diplomatically.

"They don't know everything," Sam said flatly.

"Well, they know you've served time in juvenile detention for possession of crack cocaine," Rev. Camden said. "But they took into consideration your time in rehab and the fact that it was a first offense."

Sam looked at Rev. Camden and nodded. "But do they know I can't read?" he asked, blushing with shame.

"No," Rev. Camden said. "I'm sorry—I didn't mean to put you on the spot here."

Rev. Camden took the pen from Sam's hand and pulled the application toward him.

"I'll just interview you," Rev. Camden suggested. "Then I'll fill in the blanks."

He looked the application over.

"Let's see," he said. "Your address?"

Sam cleared his throat and ran his hands through his hair again.

"I...I don't really have one," he said. "I'm staying with Barbara and her mom. That's why I need a job. You know, to carry my own weight and help pay the rent, that sort of thing."

He paused, looking at Rev. Camden intently. "I want to do the right thing," he said. "I really do."

Rev. Camden nodded. "I know you do, Sam," he replied.

"I asked Barbara to marry me," Sam said. "Did you know that?"

Rev. Camden smiled. "No," he said. "I had no idea. When's the wedding?"

"Soon," Sam said. Then he frowned. "At least, I hope," he added cautiously.

"Hope?"

"Well," Sam continued, "she said she wouldn't marry me unless I have a job, so if this is for real…"

"It's for real," Rev. Camden said.

Sam smiled, and years' worth of worry fell from his face. Rev. Camden could now see just how young the boy really was.

Young—and in for more responsibilities than he can possibly understand, Rev. Camden thought sadly.

"I don't know what to say, man," Sam continued. "Thanks for all your help."

"Don't mention it," Rev. Camden replied. "It's my job."

"And I'm going to do a great job here,"

Sam said. "I'm going to make my baby proud. I'm going to be the best table cleaner that child has ever seen. And do you know why?"

Rev. Camden shook his head.

"Because until I got involved with Barbara, I never even had a shot at cleaning tables," Sam said. "I didn't have a shot at anything until I met you and Mrs. Camden."

Rev. Camden patted Sam on the shoulder. "Let's get this form filled out," he said.

Mrs. Camden, Barbara, and Cassandra were sitting around the kitchen table, peeling carrots and cutting them into thin circles. Barbara was telling them about how she had met Sam.

"When he asked me out, I told him I was on a diet." She brushed a strand of hair away from her face. "So he said he'd take me to a sushi bar." She sighed. "I figured I wouldn't gain any weight eating raw fish." Barbara looked down at her belly. "Guess I was wrong," she whispered, forcing a smile.

"So what are you going to do?" Mrs. Camden asked. "About Sam, I mean."

"I told Sam I wouldn't marry him

unless he got a job," she said. "But the truth is, I don't want to marry him, no matter what he does."

Mrs. Camden looked up from her work.

"I'm only sixteen," Barbara said. "And he's a twenty-year-old guy with a criminal record."

Mrs. Camden began chopping again. "Well, I think Rev. Camden found him a job," she said.

But Barbara waved her hand. "Believe me," she said, "that's just not possible. That's why I used the job thing as my condition."

Mrs. Camden nodded and chopped the vegetables even faster. "But what about your baby?"

"Yeah," Barbara said dismissively. "It's a shame. Of course the baby deserves a father. And Sam *is* the father. But I don't want him to be my husband. I don't love him. I think I only said I did as an excuse to have some fun..."

Mrs. Camden grabbed a handful of peeled carrots and began to chop them into thick slices that rolled all over the table.

"Hey," Cassandra said, "if the Reverend

got Sam a job, he can get him *out* of a job!"

Mrs. Camden stopped chopping.

"You don't have to marry Sam if you don't want to," Cassandra added. "Right, Annie?"

"No—yes—I mean no," Mrs. Camden stammered. "What I mean is, you don't have to marry him, but he still might want to keep that job." She patted Barbara's hand. "Babies like to have food and shelter," she explained patiently. "They're funny that way."

Then Cassandra spoke.

"I wonder how the Reverend is going to do with crazy Roger," she said.

"Crazy Roger?" Mrs. Camden said. "Who's…"

"Roger Phillips, my ex-boyfriend," Cassandra said. "He has a temper like nothing I've ever seen."

Mrs. Camden frowned. "I hardly think asking Roger to hold your hand during the birth of his child is anything to get mad about."

Cassandra rolled her eyes. "That's not what's going to make him mad."

"I don't understand," Mrs. Camden said. "Then what will?"

"He doesn't know I'm having his child," Cassandra said. "Or any child, for that matter."

"You mean—"

Cassandra faced Mrs. Camden and nodded. "He doesn't know I'm pregnant."

Barbara reached out and touched Cassandra's arm. "Why haven't you told him?"

Cassandra sighed. "I can't. He's too mad at me for going out with his brother."

Barbara sat back in her chair.

"Whew," she said. "And I thought *I* had problems."

"Well, Reverend Camden," Sam said, standing and clutching the application in his hands. "I guess I'll introduce myself to the manager and deliver this."

"Good luck," Rev. Camden said, slapping him on the back.

"Excuse me," a voice called.

Rev. Camden turned. A sharp-eyed youth with hard features stared at him.

"I'm Roger Phillips," said the youth. "Cassandra called me and said some Reverend guy wanted to see me."

Rev. Camden shook the young man's hand. The youth stared at him warily.

"I'm Eric Camden," he said. "I guess I'm the Reverend guy...down at Glenoak Church."

"I don't go to church," Roger said. "I don't need no church."

"Well, this isn't really about church anyway," Rev. Camden explained. "My wife is volunteering at a class with Cassandra down at the community center."

"And?" Roger said impatiently.

"And Cassandra was wondering..." Rev. Camden paused. "Actually, *hoping* that you'd be interested in joining us."

"Look, pal," Roger insisted, his irritation growing. "I told you I'm not a religious guy, and I'm not interested in learning anything about religion."

"I think you—"

"I don't *want* to go to church," Roger stated emphatically. "I only came down here because a friend of mine saw Cassandra and said she looked sick or something." Roger paused. When he spoke again, his tone was softer and less hostile. "I thought maybe you were the guy they sent to tell me she was sick or dying or something."

"Would you care if she was sick?" Rev. Camden asked.

"Even though Cassandra is not one of my favorite people right now, I'd be somewhat upset if she croaked," Roger said, the edge back in his voice.

"Somewhat," Rev. Camden said.

"Okay," Roger conceded. "I'd definitely be upset— but she dated my brother, and I can't forgive her for that."

Just then, Sam returned with a big smile on his face. "Hey, Reverend," he cried, "I think I got the job!"

"That's great, but—"

Before Rev. Camden could stop him, Sam turned and faced Roger.

"So," he said, thrusting out his hand. "You must be the father of Cassandra's baby. Congratulations."

Roger did not shake Sam's hand. Instead, he stood shocked by the revelation that Cassandra was pregnant—and with his child.

Roger sat down, his mouth wide with disbelief. Rev. Camden moved to console him.

Matt entered his room, his hands filled with books. He threw the stuff on the bed and was startled to see Mary waiting for him.

"I thought you had a driver's license now," Matt said. "I'm not giving you a ride."

"I don't need a ride," Mary said. "But thanks anyway," she said sarcastically.

"I'm actually curious about how you pulled the license thing off," Matt continued. "Seems to me your parallel parking skills left something to be desired."

"Forget I was in here," Mary said, rising to leave.

But Matt stopped her. "Hey, wait," he said. "I'm sorry. I'm just in a bad mood because of this project...or lack thereof."

Mary returned and sat down across from her brother.

"I'm starting to feel like there's something wrong with me because I don't have anything to say about sex," Matt confessed.

"That's 'cause you're a guy," Mary said.

"You don't think guys have emotions?" Matt said.

"It's not that," Mary replied. "It all comes down to one basic biological fact. We women have the babies."

Matt nodded. "What was I thinking, bringing this subject up with my baby sister—?"

"I'm hardly a baby!" Mary insisted.

"Okay," Matt relented. "My little sister. Even though I know you and Lucy talk about sex all the time.

"Just forget it," Mary cried. She rose and stormed out of the room.

"What did I say?" Matt wondered out loud.

Fifteen minutes later, Matt heard a knock at his door.

"Enter the land of the uninspired," he called.

The door swung open, and Lucy walked in.

"Don't tell me *you* need a ride somewhere," Matt said.

Lucy shook her head. "Nowhere," she replied.

"Tell me," Matt said. "Isn't it true that you and Mary talk about sex all the time?"

Lucy laughed and tossed her head.

"Not all the time," she insisted. "Sometimes we talk about what we're going to have for dinner."

"Come on, tell me the truth," Matt said. "The whole sleepover thing is just a cover, right? Mary is really sneaking out with some guy, isn't she?"

"No," Lucy said. "Mary is definitely

going to a sleepover."

Matt smiled. Her answer reassured him. He knew he could always trust Lucy for the truth.

"So what can I do for you?" he asked, sitting back in his chair and throwing his legs up on the overcrowded desk. "You wanna talk about something?"

"Oh, yeah," Lucy said, thinking fast. "Do you know where Jordan and I can get a good burger tonight?"

Matt blinked. "Try the Dairy Shack," he said.

Lucy nodded and turned to leave.

"That's it?" Matt asked, surprised.

Lucy paused at the doorway. Then she stepped back into Matt's room and closed the door.

"Well, I was just thinking about your project," Lucy whispered. "Maybe you could do something on first-time experiences. Where, when, why...stuff like that."

Matt sat up and thought about it. Then he smiled brightly.

"Hey!" he cried. "That's not a bad idea. In fact, that's a great idea. I can't believe you came up with it."

"Why?" Lucy said, a little insulted. "I'm not a kid anymore. I'm fifteen. I have a —

boyfriend. I'm not *completely* naive. I do know a thing or two about life."

"Sorry," Matt replied. "But what are you getting all defensive about? I said it was a great idea." Matt grabbed his notebook off the desk and started writing intently. Lucy continued to wait by the door for a moment. Finally, Matt looked up at her again.

"What?" Matt said.

"Nothing," Lucy replied, her voice filled with disappointment. "You're welcome."

With that, she opened the door and left the room.

SIX

"I'll get it," Mrs. Camden called when she heard the doorbell. She opened the front door to find Jordan standing on the doorstep. Cassandra and Barbara peeked into the foyer from the kitchen, and giggled when they saw Jordan.

"He's cute," Cassandra whispered.

Barbara nodded. "What a hunk."

Lucy ran downstairs to meet her date. Mrs. Camden was a bit surprised at her daughter's outfit. Instead of jeans and a comfortable sweatshirt, Lucy was wearing a black skirt.

That short skirt is a little too short, Mrs. Camden decided.

"Okay, Mom," Lucy announced, throwing herself between her mother and Jordan. "I guess we'll be going."

Lucy tried to push Jordan out the door, but he wouldn't budge. "Is there anything I can do for you before we leave?" Jordan said to Mrs. Camden.

She smiled. "That's very polite of you, Jordan."

"Yeah, he's real polite, Mom," Lucy said, edging him toward the door.

"So it's the Dairy Shack and then bowling with friends?" Mrs. Camden asked.

"If that's okay with you," Jordan replied.

"Sounds like a lot of fun," Mrs. Camden said. "Have a good time."

This time, Lucy literally pushed Jordan out the door.

"Don't forget," Mrs. Camden called. "Curfew is eleven."

Lucy stopped and frowned. Jordan took her hand. "Eleven is fine," he said.

Mrs. Camden shot Lucy a look as if to tell her that she knew she was up to something.

"If you want to come in and watch a little television until midnight, that would be okay," Mrs. Camden told Jordan. "And we have freshly baked cookies."

He smiled brightly. "Thanks, Mrs. Camden," he said. "Thanks a lot."

"Yeah, Mom," Lucy said. "Thanks a lot," she repeated, closing the door behind her. "Just so you know," Lucy said to Jordan. "We are *not* going bowling."

Just then, the front door flew open again. Lucy jumped, fearing her mother had overheard her. But it was Mary. Her knapsack hung on her shoulder, and her sleeping bag was slung over her back.

"Hey," she called. "Could you guys drop me off?"

Lucy halted. "I thought Mom and her new teen friends were going to drop you off."

Lucy knew that Mary didn't want their mother anywhere near the sleepover. Mary's eyes flashed as she shot Lucy an angry look. "I told her that I was sure Jordan wouldn't mind saving her the trouble," Mary said.

"That's totally fine," Jordan said. "Hop in, Mary."

The sisters glared at each other as they got into Jordan's car. Mary sat in the back seat, Lucy in the passenger seat.

"Oh, sorry about what I said in front of Mom," Lucy said. "I didn't realize that if she took you to the sleepover she'd find out you were lying."

Jordan looked at Lucy. "And, evidently, so are *we*," he said. "So maybe we should just get out of here." He started the engine.

"What are *you* guys lying about?" Mary asked.

"We're not going bowling," Jordan replied, pulling out of the driveway.

Mary looked suddenly interested. "And why not?"

"I have no idea," he replied.

Lucy nudged Jordan with her elbow.

"What?" he cried.

Lucy pointed her thumb at Mary in the back seat. "I don't tell her everything, you know," she hissed.

Jordan halted at a stop sign. He looked at Lucy and then into the rearview mirror at Mary. Both girls were fuming.

"*This* should be a fun ride," Jordan mumbled.

Lucy resisted the urge to elbow her boyfriend again.

Simon took a stack of flat, brightly colored boxes out of the closet. He looked at the one on top. The monocled Monopoly man stared back at him.

"Too old," he decided, pushing the box aside.

He looked at the next box and shook his head. "Who cares who killed who?" Simon said as he threw the Clue box on the discard pile.

"Bingo," Simon said, shaking his head again. "We need more than two players to make Bingo fun."

Simon smiled as he lifted the next box. Just then, Mrs. Camden entered his bedroom.

"Mary and Lucy have gone out," she informed him. "Are you ready for your first big night as a professional baby-sitter?"

Simon smiled and held up the box in his hand.

"They told us in baby-sitting class that kids love board games," he explained. "I thought I'd see if Ruthie is interested in any of this stuff."

Mrs. Camden frowned. "I think Ruthie got tired of Chutes and Ladders a couple years ago," she said.

Simon glanced again at the game in his hand.

"Of course," he added. "Whatever Ruthie wants to do is fine with me."

Mrs. Camden looked horrified.

"No, no!" she cried. "You don't want to *just* do whatever Ruthie wants to do."

Simon looked bewildered.

"Let me explain," she said, sitting down next to him on the bed. "Tonight, you're not her brother, and you're not her friend, either."

"I'm *not?*"

"Tonight, you are a surrogate parent," Mrs. Camden said. "And your job is to see that Ruthie is safe, that her basic needs are met, and beyond that, that she has a little clean and safe fun—but not at your expense."

Simon nodded.

"She didn't already con you into the 'we have to do whatever I want' bit, did she?" Mrs. Camden asked.

"Of course not!" Simon lied. "Give me a little credit, Mom. I'm smarter than that."

"Good." Mrs. Camden smiled and handed Simon a piece of paper. "Here is the number at the pool hall," she said. "We're only five minutes away if you get into any trouble. And, of course, Matt is upstairs—"

"Mom!" Simon cried. "I want to do this alone!"

"Don't worry," she assured him. "Matt

doesn't want to be bothered unless it's an emergency."

"Why is he home at all?" Simon asked, obviously disappointed.

"He's working on his project," Mrs. Camden explained. "But don't worry. Matt is way up in the attic. Ruthie doesn't even know he's home, or she'd be bothering him already."

"Okay, I guess," Simon replied, not very happy about how things were working out. "I suppose beggars can't be choosers. And I need all the experience I can get."

Mrs. Camden kissed Simon on the cheek.

"Hey, come on, Mom," he protested. "I'm working here."

"Sorry," Mrs. Camden said, smiling.

Matt leaned back in his chair and cranked up the volume in his headphones. He pondered Lucy's suggestion. His initial enthusiasm for the idea had long since worn off in the face of some practical considerations.

Where am I going to find a bunch of people this weekend who are willing to talk on tape about their first-time experiences? Matt wondered.

He knew Lucy's idea was good. But

Matt felt there was something missing with the concept. And he couldn't quite put his finger on it.

He threw his feet up on the desk and leaned back. With his hands behind his head, Matt let the music wash over him, still hoping for inspiration.

Ruthie was gathering up her dolls for a tea party when she heard a knock at the door.

"Can I come in?" Mrs. Camden asked.

"Enter," Ruthie said as her mother opened the door. "You look positively divine!" Ruthie told her mother.

"Why, thank you," Mrs. Camden said, modeling her outfit in the doorway. "It's my first time out in a long time. I wanted to look nice."

"I hope you have a lot of fun," Ruthie said, returning to her dolls. Mrs. Camden stepped into the little girl's room.

"We'll be back in a couple of hours," Mrs. Camden said. "So you be good."

"Stay out as late as you want," Ruthie said, not looking up from her tea set.

Mrs. Camden gave her youngest daughter a serious look. "You're not going to give Simon a hard time, are you?" she asked, hands on hips.

"Me?" Ruthie cried. "When have I ever given a baby-sitter any trouble?"

She looked up at her mother, an angelic expression on her face.

But Mrs. Camden didn't buy it for a minute.

"You *bit* Matt the first time he baby-sat you," Mrs. Camden reminded her. "Hard."

Ruthie shrugged. "I was mad you left me at home. But I've grown up since then."

"The first time Mary baby-sat you, I came home to find her locked in the linen closet," Mrs. Camden continued.

"She wouldn't leave me alone!" Ruthie cried. "She was driving me crazy with all those stupid board games." Ruthie looked up at her. "How many times would *you* want to play Chutes and Ladders?"

Mrs. Camden nodded. "Point taken," she said. "But what about the last time Lucy was supposed to keep an eye on you—?"

Ruthie looked away with a guilty expression.

"You and Simon left the house, followed the mailman, and got completely lost."

Ruthie crossed her heart. "I promise we won't leave the house."

Mrs. Camden was sure that something was up with each of the Camden girls tonight, but she didn't have time to handle it. She had to take Barbara and Cassandra down to the pool hall, and they were already late.

"Okay," she sighed. "But really, Ruthie, go easy on Simon. He's a good brother."

Ruthie smiled like a cat and hugged her mother. Mrs. Camden kissed her and quickly left the room.

When she was gone, Ruthie rubbed her hands together like a cartoon villain bent on mischief.

"Oh boy, oh boy, oh boy…" she whispered to herself.

Jordan parked the car in front of the Caldwell house. Mary climbed out of the back seat and threw her knapsack and sleeping bag over her shoulder.

"Thanks, Jordan," she said.

"Don't mention it," he replied. Lucy kept her eyes in front of her, completely avoiding her sister. As the car drove off, Mary turned and walked up the long sidewalk to the house.

The Caldwells lived in the nicest part of Glenoak. Their house was large and shaded by lots of trees. It even had a pool in the backyard, and Tina, the Caldwell's daughter and Mary's teammate, was a competitive swimmer.

Mary rang the doorbell.

Lauren Michaels and Jason Patterson opened the door.

"Hey, Mary!" Jason cried.

"Join the parteeeeee!" Lauren shouted.

Music blared out from behind them. It looked as if this particular sleepover was taking place in the Caldwell's living room, not the basement.

Mary's mouth opened in surprise. "What's going on?" she asked, confused.

"Haven't you heard?" Lauren said. "The Caldwells had a family emergency. Mr. and Mrs. Caldwell had to leave town this afternoon. Tina's here all alone, except for us."

"Yeah!" Jason chimed in. "We've got the place to ourselves. No chaperones!"

Mary smiled weakly.

"Come on in," Jason insisted. "Frank Malone'll be here any minute. He really likes you. And you two can be alone!"

Mary's mouth dropped open. *Frank Malone likes me?* she thought. This was news to her.

"If there are any rooms left to be alone," Lauren added, waving behind her. "It's even wilder than McArthur's Point in here tonight."

Lauren and Jason both laughed and wandered away. Mary walked into the house and looked around. The living room was dark. The dance music had just been replaced with a slow number. Couples began dancing in the dark.

Some of them were kissing.

Mary tapped her fingers nervously on the staircase. There was no sign of her close friends. Or anyone she could trust. Mary was beginning to get nervous now. Really, really nervous.

Rev. Camden pretended to watch Sam as he lined up another shot on the pool table. But his eyes were really on Roger Phillips.

I had no idea he would react like that, Rev. Camden thought. *But then again, I thought he had some idea of what I wanted to talk about.*

He shook his head sadly.

Ever since he heard the news, Roger Phillips had been fuming. After he got over his initial shock, he spent half an hour pacing back and forth, his eyes glued to the poolhall's entrance. He was obviously waiting for Cassandra to come through the door.

After Sam made his shot, Rev. Camden approached Roger. He put his hand on the boy's shoulder. "If you want to go home and let some of the shock wear off before you see Cassandra, that would be fine," he said. "You really don't have to hang out here."

Roger whirled around and faced Rev. Camden. "No!" he said angrily. "I'm not going home until I have a word with her." He paused for a moment. "Actually, until I have a *lot* of words with her," he said.

Rev. Camden held up his hand. "But *careful* words," he suggested gently.

Roger glared at him.

"You see," Rev. Camden continued. "Someday, Cassandra may tell your child what you said when *you* found out you were having a baby. And those words will stay with your child forever." Rev. Camden paused and looked into Roger's eyes. "So if I were you, I would…"

Roger stared past Rev. Camden, no longer hearing him. The Reverend turned to see his wife entering the pool hall. Barbara and Cassandra trailed behind her.

Mrs. Camden saw her husband and approached.

"Sweetie!" Sam cried when he saw Barbara. He ran over and grabbed the girl and whirled her around in his arms.

"I got the job!" he cried excitedly.

"Congratulations," Barbara mumbled, pushing away from him.

Mrs. Camden watched Barbara and Sam. But Rev. Camden kept his eyes on Cassandra as she cautiously approached Roger.

"You!" Roger screamed when he saw her. "How could you!"

To everyone's shock, Roger Phillips broke down and cried right in the middle of the pool hall.

The room grew suddenly silent as Cassandra backed away from him, tears welling up in her eyes, too.

Lucy followed Jordan into the Dairy Shack. They had some trouble finding a parking place and weren't surprised to see that the burger joint was jammed with the usual Friday night crowd—teens from the local high schools. Lucy saw a few of her friends and waved to them. Lucy's friend Pamela noticed Lucy's short skirt and winked.

"Hey, Lucy! Hey, Jordan!" voices called from across the restaurant. The couple turned to see Jordan's friends Gary, Hutch, and Darrell. They were sitting in a booth in the far corner of the diner. Jordan waved to his friends and led Lucy over to meet them. Like Jordan, most of his friends were seniors and varsity athletes. They knew Mary pretty well, but had never spoken to Lucy before.

"Nice outfit," Gary said. Lucy smiled at the compliment.

"Are you guys going bowling later?" Darrell asked, noting that Lucy was hardly dressed for bowling.

"Or is it the pool hall?" he said.

"Maybe," Jordan replied.

"We're going someplace special," Lucy said.

"Like where?" Darrell asked.

"Don't know," Jordan replied, shrugging. "It's news to me, too."

"We just want to be alone tonight," Lucy said.

"Whoa." Gary whistled suggestively. "Alone…where? Like at McArthur's Point, maybe?"

Jordan blushed. "No way," he said, dismissing the notion with a wave of his hand.

"Do you know what Lucy's dad would do to me if I took his daughter there?"

Lucy elbowed Jordan in an attempt to shut him up.

"Don't be so hasty," she said. "McArthur's Point might be fun."

"Darrell was supposed to go to the basketball sleepover," Gary said, changing the subject. "But his parents found out that it's co-ed."

"How could they not know?" Hutch wondered out loud.

"'Cause I didn't tell them," Darrell said softly. "I didn't think I was doing anything wrong."

"Then why didn't you tell your parents the truth?" Gary demanded. "If you thought it was okay, why'd you hide the fact that boys *and* girls were going to be there?"

Darrell shrugged, at a loss for a reply.

"Anyway," Gary said, "I heard the whole sleepover might be canceled. The Caldwells had a family emergency and had to go out of town this weekend."

"Who knows what I might have missed?" Darrell said, throwing up his hands.

"Forget about it," Gary said, poking his

friend. "We'll have more fun at the bowling alley."

"Are you sure you're not coming tonight?" Hutch asked Jordan and Lucy.

"Maybe we'll show up later," Jordan said.

The conversation shifted to the local varsity basketball teams and the upcoming playoffs. Lucy was quickly bored by sports talk and dragged Jordan away from his friends.

"Let's get something to eat," she suggested. "I'm famished."

They got in line. "Welcome to Dairy Shack," Arnold, a young member of Rev. Camden's church, greeted them from behind the counter.

"Hi, Arnold," Lucy said unenthusiastically.

"So," Arnold said, adjusting his paper hat, "what can I get for you? We have some specials today. Fish and chips with malt vinegar...Chicken tenders with the Dairy Shack's special sauce...How about our black-and-white milkshake? It's two for the price of one on Fridays..."

Jordan turned to Lucy. "The usual?" he asked.

She nodded.

"We'll take two burgers with everything on them," Jordan replied. "Add fries and a couple of Cokes."

Arnold nodded, writing the order down on his yellow pad.

"For here or to go?"

"For here," Jordan replied.

Suddenly, he got another elbow in his ribs. Jordan rubbed his side.

"Make the order to go," Lucy said, stepping up to the counter.

"Go?" Jordan said. "Go…where?"

Lucy smiled up at him. "Can't we just park someplace and eat in the car?" she asked.

"Park…where?" Jordan replied. He thought he knew what Lucy had in mind, but he wanted to hear her say it.

"What about McArthur's Point?" Lucy suggested. "Isn't that where everyone else goes to get away from other people?"

Jordan studied Lucy. "I don't think your parents would approve of that," he said.

"I *know* they wouldn't," Arnold added.

Lucy shot the clerk a hard look and then faced her date. "He recently joined our church," Lucy said, motioning to Arnold. "And he's gone a little overboard on the religion thing."

"It's not safe at McArthur's Point," Jordan said. "It's not safe to park on a dark road anywhere. You never know what kind of lunatics are out there."

"But I feel safe with you," Lucy replied.

Jordan wouldn't give in. "Make it for here," he told Arnold. The clerk smiled.

While Arnold was getting their order, Lucy faced Jordan. "Don't you find me attractive?" she asked with sadness in her voice.

Jordan was shocked by the question. "Of course I do!" he said.

"Well?" she persisted. "Why can't we go to McArthur's Point, then?"

Jordan shook his head. "The last thing I want to do is take you to some make-out place in the woods."

"Am I that ugly?" Lucy demanded.

"No, but—"

"But you just don't want to be alone with me?"

Jordan looked trapped. "That's not what I meant!"

"Then what, exactly, *did* you mean?" Lucy demanded. "You obviously went to McArthur's Point—or somewhere—with *another* girl. What, was she prettier than me?"

"Let's get a table and talk," Jordan said with one eye on Arnold, who could hear their entire conversation.

"Can we talk about going somewhere where we can be alone?" Lucy said.

Jordan laughed. Lucy was not amused.

"This is not funny to me," she said.

"Hey," Jordan said. "I'm older than you are. I'm bigger than you are. And you can't pressure me into doing anything I don't want to do," he said, smiling.

"I don't even know what I want to do!" Lucy said. "But I would like to feel like you're at least a little bit attracted to me."

Jordan stared at Lucy, who stared right back at him. Arnold handed them a tray full of food. Jordan looked at the tray, then at Lucy again. He paused for a moment.

"Make it to go," he said.

Lucy smiled at Alex and wrapped her arm around his. She saw the disapproving stare on the clerk's face. "Shut up, Arnold," Lucy said.

Arnold stuffed the order into two big bags. Jordan paid for it.

"Let's go," Lucy said. "I'm dying of hunger."

"If your mom and dad find out about this, we'll both be *dead*," Jordan declared.

SEVEN

Mary slouched in a chair in a darkened corner of the Caldwells' living room, praying for invisibility. The doorbell rang, and she looked up hopefully. Two guys Mary didn't even know had arrived.

"Hey, Carlos and Vincent are here!" someone shouted.

Some of the basketball players rushed up to greet the new guests.

Mary recognized their names. Carlos and Vincent were both players on the Conroy High basketball team.

What are they doing here? she wondered. *I thought this was for Walter Reed students only.*

Mary saw Carlos grab Tina Caldwell in a bear hug. As she struggled in his powerful grip, he kissed her. Vincent laughed at his partner's antics, but Tina was obviously not amused.

The music changed, the lights grew even dimmer, and more couples paired up to dance. Mary watched from a distance. She saw one of her teammates on the couch with her boyfriend. They were acting like they were at McArthur's Point, not in a room full of people.

"I can't watch this," Mary muttered.

She got up and went into the kitchen, where there was a huge spread of food. A selection of lunch meats, soft drinks, potato chips, and other snacks littered the counter. She poured herself a tall glass of milk and started making a sandwich.

Suddenly, she felt strong arms wrap around her.

Mary turned. Vincent had grabbed her, and he wouldn't let go.

"Hey!" Mary cried. "Watch the hands, buster."

She tried to make light of the stranger's behavior, but Vincent still wouldn't let her loose.

"Hey, you're Mary Camden," he said. "I've totally got the hots for you."

"So what?" Mary said, trying to squirm

out of his grip. But the more she resisted, the closer Vincent held her.

"Give me a kiss," Vincent demanded, squeezing her tighter. Mary fought against him, but he was too strong.

"How about another round of Chutes and Ladders?" Simon suggested hopefully.

Ruthie stared at him as if he had a disease.

"Are you crazy!" the little girl cried. "I thought we were going to do what *I* wanted to do!"

"I thought you *wanted* to play Chutes and Ladders." Simon was already losing his cool.

"No!" Ruthie said. "Not at all."

Simon rolled his eyes. "So what *do* you want to do?" he asked.

Ruthie put one finger under her chin as she thought about it.

"I want to rollerblade," she said after a long pause.

"But you promised Mom that you wouldn't leave the house," Simon said, almost pleading.

"You're right," Ruthie said. "I guess that means you'll have to create a roller rink for me right here in the living room."

"I can't do that," Simon said.

"Then I'll just scream and scream until the neighbors can hear me," Ruthie said, crossing her arms and taking a deep breath.

Simon jumped up and covered her mouth. "Okay, okay," he said. "Go get your skates."

Once Ruthie was gone, Simon rubbed his face with his hands.

I hope baby-sitting isn't always this hard, he thought.

"You've got about one second to let go of me!" Mary cried.

Vincent chuckled and let her go.

Mary stepped back, almost spilling her milk. "What kind of a jerk are you, anyway?"

"Hey," Vincent said, his pride wounded. "Tina said her parents weren't around and that this party would be fun."

"Fun doesn't mean pawing every girl in the place," Mary insisted. "What makes you think any of us *want* to be pawed by you or anybody else?"

"Well, you're here, aren't you?" Vincent shot back.

"What's that supposed to mean?" Mary

said.

"It's a co-ed sleepover," he replied. "The only reason to come is to play with the opposite sex."

Mary rolled her eyes. "Oh, so if the lights are dim and there's romantic music, then everything is okay?"

Vincent shrugged and popped a chip into his mouth. "Yeah," he replied. "Something like that."

"If *that's* what you think, then you're plain dumb," Mary said.

A couple suddenly stumbled into the kitchen. It was Carlos and Rita, a girl from Mary's team. The boy's arms were around the girl, and she was giggling excitedly.

"We can be alone now," Carlos whispered to Rita, pushing her toward the cellar door. Rita giggled again and allowed herself to be led to the basement.

When they were gone, Vincent shot his thumb in the departing couple's direction. "I wonder who's really being plain dumb?" he said.

Mary glared at him.

"Why come to an all-night, co-ed sleepover otherwise?" Vincent said over his shoulder as he left the kitchen.

Mary picked up her plate and looked at

the sandwich she'd made for herself. She discovered that she'd all but lost her appetite.

Ruthie swerved to avoid the table in the foyer. But as she rolled past it, she bumped one of its legs with her rollerblade. As Simon watched in horror, a vase on the table tilted, but then miraculously balanced itself.

"Whew," Simon cried. "That was close."

Ruthie skated on madly. She decided to leave the course Simon had laid out for her. Instead of circling the inner edge of the rug, Ruthie was now taking off across the hardwood floor. She rolled into the living room, and then the dining room.

"Stay on the rug!" Simon pleaded.

"I can't!" Ruthie replied.

"Why not?"

"Because then I can't go fast," said the little girl.

"Ruthie," Simon called, "slow down this instant!"

"But that's no fun. I need to be *free*," Ruthie said, shooting past him, her curly hair trailing from under her safety helmet.

She rolled around the living room, then

turned and flashed past Simon again. He reached out to catch her, but Ruthie was too fast.

"Oh, no!" Simon cried.

"Help!" Ruthie yelped. She had lost control and was rolling toward the end table next to the living room couch.

Simon lurched after her. His move was so sudden that he ended up tripping over his own feet.

"Watch out!" Simon called as he struck the floor.

But his breathless warning came too late. Ruthie slammed headfirst into the table. There was a loud crack as helmet struck wood. The little girl bounced backward and hit the floor.

Ruthie giggled insanely. "What a trip!" she cried.

The force of the impact knocked a lamp off the end table. It tumbled onto the sofa and the bulb popped. The living room went dark.

Simon scrambled to his feet and rushed across the room. To Ruthie's surprise, he ignored her and proceeded directly to the overhead light switch.

As light filled the room, Simon saw that glass was everywhere. Luckily, the lamp was not damaged. Simon gently placed it back on the end table and went to get the broom and dustpan.

Ruthie struggled to her knees, then to her feet. She watched Simon as he cleaned up the glass and replaced the light bulb.

"You're supposed to baby-sit *me*," she insisted. "Not the stupid lamp."

"You could've been hurt," Simon said. "That wasn't very smart."

"I'm a little girl." Ruthie grinned. "I don't have to be smart."

"Oh, no!" Simon cried, looking at the floor. Across the shiny hardwood surface, from the foyer to the dining room, Ruthie's wheels had left black rubber marks.

"I told you to stay on the rug!" Simon yelled.

Ruthie didn't like the tone of his voice and decided to ignore him. She took off again, gaining speed as her wheels hit the bare hardwood floor once more.

Simon dropped the broom and ran to the kitchen closet. He found floor wax and a bunch of rags. For the next half hour, he followed Ruthie around the room, using the floor polish to clean up the trail of rubber she left behind.

"This is fun!" Ruthie said, skidding to a

halt.

"That's it!" Simon cried, grabbing her. Ruthie's legs shot out from under her as Simon slammed his sister into an easy chair.

"Take off those skates," he demanded.

Ruthie decided not to push it, so she took off her rollerblades. But she didn't give up without an argument. "You promised we'd do anything I wanted," she said. "And I wanted to skate."

"And I made you a nice course on the rug," Simon said.

"Not on the rug!" Ruthie howled. "I want to feel the breeze in my face."

"Well, then...want something else," Simon said as he threw her rollerblades into the corner. "Because this is only going to get both of us in big trouble."

"I won't get in any trouble," Ruthie said, her nose held high. "*I'm* not the baby-sitter."

Simon dropped to his knees. "Please, Ruthie," he begged. "Pretty, pretty, pretty please."

"Okay," Ruthie replied, looking around. "Why don't we jump rope?"

"Because we promised Mom we wouldn't go out of the house," Simon explained, his patience wearing thin.

Ruthie pointed to the foyer. "We could do it there," she said.

Simon shook his head doubtfully.

"You could tie one end of the rope to the banister and you could hold the other end," Ruthie suggested.

Simon checked it out. "There's not enough room," he announced. "We might break something."

Ruthie pointed to the table. "Move that!" she said. "Then there will be plenty of room."

"Fine!" Simon said, his shoulders sagging.

"I'll go and get my rope," Ruthie screamed, jumping up and down a few times. "You're the best baby-sitter I've ever had."

Simon smiled as he watched his sister run up the steps. Then he put his full weight against the heavy table. It wouldn't budge.

Just then, Matt came down the stairs. He walked past Simon, who still struggled with the table.

"A little help, please?" Simon asked.

"I can't stop," Matt said, heading for the kitchen. "I'm really into this project, and I don't want to lose my train of thought."

"Of course not!" Simon called after him. "I'm sure those trains don't come along too often." Simon pushed the table again. It wouldn't move an inch.

Ruthie returned, jump rope in hand.

"Sorry," Simon said apologetically. "I don't think it's going to work—the table won't budge."

Ruthie joined Simon. Together, they pushed the table, but it remained in place.

"I guess we'll have to do something else," Simon said, sighing. "Maybe I could read to you in your room?"

Ruthie rolled her eyes. "That's not a plan!"

"Well, then," Simon said, "what do you want to do?"

Ruthie thought about it. A sly smile appeared on her face. "We could play cops and robbers," she said.

A look of suspicion crossed Simon's face. "How do you play that, according to Ruthie Camden?" he asked.

"I'll be the cop," Ruthie said. "And you be the robber."

"You don't have handcuffs, do you?"

"No, silly." Ruthie shook her head. "But

this rope might come in handy."

Simon rolled his eyes. "I have a bad feeling about this."

Mary was hiding in a walk-in closet when she heard a familiar voice. She jumped to her feet and opened the closet door a crack. She saw Frank on the far side of the living room talking to one of his friends.

"Hey, Frank," Mary whispered. "Over here."

Mary didn't know much about Frank Malone. He'd transferred to Walter Reed from California last year. His family went to her father's church, but Frank didn't talk much—at church or at school.

Though Frank was an athlete, he seemed to be more interested in computers and his studies. Mary had never thought of Frank as her "type" before.

"Hey Frank...Frank Malone!" Mary called. "Over here."

Frank looked around a moment before he spotted her.

"Mary!" Frank said, surprised. He crossed the room. "I...I didn't know you'd be here."

He looked around the living room, his handsome face clouded by distaste. "This is my first sleepover," he said. "Is it always like this?"

"Tina Caldwell's parents went out of town," Mary explained. "So the animals are in charge of the zoo."

To Frank's surprise, Mary's hand shot out. She grabbed his shirt and dragged him into the closet with her.

"What are you doing?" he asked, blushing. Frank seemed really uncomfortable with girls, Mary noted.

"'Shhh!" Mary demanded, putting her hand over his mouth. "I'm hiding," she explained.

"Hiding?" Frank said, totally confused.

Mary pushed him down on her sleeping bag, then sat down next to him.

"I was…uncomfortable," Mary confessed. "I know you're practically a stranger, but you go to our church, so…" Her voice trailed off. Then she shivered. "This party is giving me the creeps."

Frank nodded. "Tina should have canceled it when her parents went out of town."

"Maybe her parents thought she did," Mary said.

"Yeah, maybe," Frank agreed. He looked at Mary, who was looking straight back at him. "Maybe we should leave," he suggested.

Mary shook her head vigorously.

"I can't go home," she said, her voice barely above a whisper. "What would I tell my mom? That things got out of hand? That the boys were all over the girls? Boys aren't even supposed to *be* here, as far as she knows."

"I think some of the girls are all over the guys, too," Frank added.

"Whatever," Mary replied.

"So what do we do?" he asked. "Stay in the closet all night?"

Mary looked at him, her eyes pleading.

"Okay, okay," Frank said. "But if things quiet down, we're going back out in the living room."

Mary looked at Frank Malone. She could see that he enjoyed talking to her, but it was obvious that he wasn't happy about the circumstances.

Maybe he's just shy, Mary thought.

"I just don't get it," she said sadly. "We've had lots of sleepovers. But nothing like this ever happened before."

"I guess I'm not really surprised," Frank confessed.

"Huh?"

"I never would have come here if I'd known Tina's parents weren't going to chaperone," Frank continued. "It's guys and girls spending the night together. *And* no parents are around to watch things. Don't you see anything *wrong* with that?"

"No," Mary said. "Not at all. I think it's just good fun."

"To *you*, maybe."

"What's that supposed to mean?" Mary asked.

Frank shrugged. "Just because you think things are harmless, it doesn't mean they are," he explained. "It's perception versus reality."

"I still don't get it."

"Your perception is that we're all here for some innocent fun, even though the situation is a little questionable," Frank said. "But the reality is that some of the guys— and some of the girls, too—are here for another, not-so-innocent reason."

He paused. "You may not like it," Frank said at last. "But that's the reality."

Mary nodded, finally understanding. "Perception versus reality," she said.

"And reality always wins," Frank added.

Then he looked at Mary's knapsack.

"You got anything to eat in there?" he asked, pointing. "I'm starving."

"I left my sandwich in the kitchen," Mary said. "But I have these."

Mary produced the cookies her mother had given her. "We can share my milk," she said as they began to eat.

Matt opened the refrigerator and snatched a plastic container of milk from the shelf. He looked around for something more satisfying.

"No cake," he muttered. "Guess I'll have to settle for a cookie." He filled his glass to the brim before bothering to check the cookie jar—he was disappointed to find it empty.

If I know Mom, she's got a stash of cookies hidden around here somewhere.

He checked the oven, the cupboard, and under the fruit basket before he found the plate of cookies in the microwave.

Aw, come on, Mom. You've got to do better than that, he said to himself.

Matt thought about Lucy's idea as he ate a few of the cookies. Interviewing people about their first-time experiences sounded good, but he was still having trouble shaping the concept into an actual project.

I wish Lucy were here, Matt thought. *If she could come up with the idea, she could probably make it work somehow. Geez, here I am struggling to come up with a project, and my high school sister gives me the idea.*

Well, Matt thought. *I guess she's more mature than I am sometimes.*

Matt swallowed hard. *No,* he thought. *She can't be—not my little sister!*

Matt's mind flashed back to the moment when Lucy had come to him with the idea. *Maybe you could do it about people's first-time experiences.* Matt smacked himself in the head.

"I'm an idiot!" he cried.

He snatched his car keys from the rack, grabbed his jacket, ran out the back door, and jumped into his car. He skidded out of the driveway, his mind on one thing and one thing only.

I've got to find Lucy before she makes the worst mistake of her life!

EIGHT

"But I *do* love you," Sam said to Barbara. Roger and Cassandra sat at another table, locked in a deep discussion. The Reverend and Mrs. Camden were seated together at a third booth. They watched the two couples hashing out their problems.

Sam reached across the table and touched Barbara's hand. She pulled away as if his touch were fire. Sam frowned and placed his hands back in his lap.

"If you loved me, you wouldn't have had sex with me when I was fifteen years old," Barbara said, her voice choked with emotion.

"No, I did that because I cared about you," Sam said.

"If you cared, you would have waited

until I was ready instead of pushing me into something I knew nothing about," Barbara continued. Her eyes were bright with tears. "Now look at me," she cried, clutching her belly. "I'm sixteen and I'm having a baby. And...I'm really scared."

"But I thought you wanted to...to do it," Sam said.

"And so what if I did?" she shot back. "You're older, and you're supposed to be smarter. You should have been looking out for me if you really loved me."

"But I'm looking out for you now," Sam said, looking into her eyes. "I've got a job. We have a future. And I'm going to marry you."

"A future?" Barbara said, laughing in his face. "You think busing tables at this pool hall for minimum wage is a *future*?" Her eyes filled with tears again. "That's not even a start," she said.

"I know things aren't perfect. But I swear I'll make them better," Sam promised. "For you. For the baby. For *us*."

Barbara began to cry.

"You only want to marry me because I'm having a baby," she sobbed. "If I weren't, you wouldn't even be thinking about it...and neither would I."

Sam looked down at the table. He had nothing to say. He knew she was absolutely right.

Roger refused to look Cassandra in the eye, even when they sat down at a table. He'd pulled himself together, but Cassandra's discomfort at his emotional outburst remained.

"It's just not fair," Roger said after a long silence. "We went out for less than six months, and now we're going to spend our whole lives together."

Cassandra looked up at Roger, her expression one of surprise. "You want to get married?" she said.

"No!" Roger barked. "I don't want to get married. Not to *you*, anyway."

"Then what?"

"Don't you get it?" Roger demanded. "The two of us made this baby, and now—whether we like it or not—we have a life-long connection to each other."

The revelation hit on Cassandra like a thunderbolt. Instantly, her eyes grew sad. Roger suddenly reached out and caressed Cassandra's cheek. She blinked in surprise at the gentleness of his touch.

"The connection is our child," Roger

said, his voice soft. "A helpless little child who had no choice at all."

Cassandra nodded as tears flowed down her cheeks.

"I guess we owe it to this baby to at least be friends," Roger continued. "And to help each other throughout this kid's life, whether we want to or not."

Cassandra reached up and touched Roger's fingers. He pulled his hand away from her face.

"How could you do it?" he said, his tone angry again. "How could you go out with my brother knowing that you were having my baby?"

Cassandra stared at him, her own anger bubbling to the surface. "I wanted to get back at you for doing this to me."

Roger shook his head. "I wonder what this kid is going to think of us for not being the family we should have been before we created it."

Cassandra blinked. "It's not an *it*," she said coolly. "He's a boy."

Roger's shoulders sagged, and he broke down into tears once more.

Mrs. Camden made a move toward Roger. But Rev. Camden reached out and stopped her.

"Leave them alone," he said. "Let them work it out on their own."

Mrs. Camden nodded, realizing that her husband was right. If they were old enough to make a baby, then they were old enough to at least try to solve this problem. The Reverend and Mrs. Camden watched the couples for a few more minutes.

"Things don't look so good," Mrs. Camden said finally.

Rev. Camden nodded. "There's really nothing good about teenage pregnancy."

"They're just not old enough," Mrs. Camden said with a sigh.

"Don't you want to kiss me?" Lucy asked.

Jordan choked and nearly dropped what was left of his Dairy Shack burger.

"Wha—what?" he stammered, taking a big gulp of his Coke to force down his food. "Sure, I want to kiss you," he said.

Jordan nervously stared out the window of his car. Lucy sat fuming beside him. They were parked at McArthur's Point. Though it was a Friday night, it was still too early for the crowd to show up. Jordan's car was the only one on the hill.

"Lucy," Jordan said, "I kiss you at the end of every date. I kiss you between classes if we run into each other in the hall. What else do you want?"

She looked at him. "Do you actually *like* kissing me?" she asked, her voice quiet.

"Of course!" Jordan cried. "I live for it. I dream of it. My life is incomplete without it."

"Stop teasing me," Lucy said, annoyed. "This is serious."

They sat in silence for a while. Then Jordan spoke. "What's this all about? You've been acting weird for the past couple of days."

"I don't know," Lucy said, nervously tapping the window with her finger. "Maybe I'm just wondering how you really feel about me."

Jordan smiled. "Well that's easy," he said. "I like you, Lucy. I like you a lot."

"So?" Lucy shrugged. "Here we are— alone at last. Why don't you kiss me?"

Jordan froze. "I don't know," he said.

"I won't bite."

Jordan laughed nervously. "Okay," he said. "Let's sit here and talk for a while. And then, when you least expect it, I'll kiss you." He looked at her again. "Is that all right?"

Lucy shrugged. "You have to *want* to

kiss me," she whispered.

"I do!" Jordan insisted.

Lucy looked her date right in the eye.

"If you *do*," she said evenly, "if you really do like kissing me, I want you to prove it right here and right now..."

Matt double-parked in front of the Dairy Shack, blocking a van full of guys from Crawford College. He cut the engine and jumped out of the car.

"Hey, Camden, is that you?" one of the guys in the van called after him.

Matt turned and waved, then bolted for the door.

"Come on, man!" the driver cried. "Move that hunk-of-junk Camaro!"

But Matt was already inside. He looked around, searching for Lucy and Jordan. There was no sign of them. As he pushed his way to the front of the line, people began to yell.

But Matt ignored them.

"Hey, look!" Darrell said, poking Gary. "Isn't that Matt Camden? Lucy's brother."

"Yeah," Hutch said, glancing up from his third milk shake. "He looks pretty mad."

"Excuse me," Matt said, cutting in

front of a pretty cheerleader.

"Hi ya, Camden!" Arnold said from behind the counter. "So you came here for your old job back or what?"

"Ha-ha," Matt replied, clearly not amused.

"What can I do you for?" Arnold asked. "You seem to be in a hurry."

"Have you seen Lucy with a tall, beefy, blond guy?"

Arnold scratched his head, not sure how Matt would react to the truth. "You mean Jordan?"

"Right!"

"Lenny," Arnold called over his shoulder to someone in the kitchen. "Take over for me. I'm gonna take five."

He led Matt to an empty table. Arnold spoke quietly so that nobody could overhear their conversation. "They were here," he began. "About an hour ago, I think."

"Are you sure?" Matt demanded.

"I took their order myself," Arnold said, nodding.

"What's up, Arnold?" Matt said. "You're not telling me something."

Arnold squirmed and pulled on the collar of his Dairy Shack uniform.

"From what they were saying, I'm

guessing they took their burgers to McArthur's Point."

Matt blinked. Arnold leaned closer to Matt and whispered into his ear. "It was your *sister's* idea, from what I overheard…"

Matt got up so fast that he knocked over his chair. Everyone in the Dairy Shack froze. Matt flew out the door.

"I'd sure hate to be Jordan right now," Arnold snickered as he watched the black Camaro fishtail out of the parking lot.

Jordan looked at Lucy, in shock that she could give him such a silly ultimatum. "Come on, Lucy," he pleaded.

"I mean it," Lucy said stubbornly. "Kiss me now like you mean it, or take me home."

"This is ridiculous!"

"To you, maybe," Lucy replied. "But to me, it's been quite revealing. You obviously aren't attracted to me, and you're dating me only because you feel sorry for me."

"You know that's not true," Jordan said. "I'm not putting the moves on you now *because* I want to date you."

"Hah!" Lucy cried. "That's a good one."

"It's true," he insisted. "If your parents found out we were here, they'd stop us from dating in a second."

Lucy crossed her arms and looked away. But she had to admit that Jordan was making some sense.

"But you've never tried to make out with me!" Lucy said. "Not even once…"

"That's because I respect you."

"That's what my sister said," Lucy shot back.

"See!" Jordan cried.

"I didn't believe her, either."

Lucy turned and faced him. "Kiss me like you mean it, or I'm going to be very disappointed in you," she said, sliding across the seat to get closer to him.

Jordan felt the heat of her body next to his. "Maybe just once," he said. His voice was hoarse, almost a whisper.

"That's all I'm asking for," Lucy said softly.

Jordan took her in his arms.

Suddenly, they heard the sound of a rapidly approaching car. Headlights washed over them. A black vehicle skidded to a halt right next to Jordan's car. For a moment, it was lost in a cloud of dust.

The dust settled, and Jordan felt hard eyes on him. He looked up. Matt Camden was glaring at him from the other car.

Jordan had never seen him so angry.

He must have seen me kissing Lucy, Jordan thought with rising panic. *Well, almost kissing Lucy…*

"Luce," Matt barked. "Get in my car. *Right now!*"

"You're busted, mister!"

Ruthie's triumphant cry rang through the house. Simon rolled his eyes.

"Okay," he said, holding his hands above his head. "I surrender. Read me my rights."

"You're under arrest," Ruthie declared, pinning Simon's arms behind his back and wrapping her jump rope around them.

"You'll never take me alive," Simon said in his best bad-guy voice.

"Too late," Ruthie said. "I've already got you." Ruthie led Simon over to the staircase in the foyer. "Sit down," she commanded. "I have to intricate you."

"You mean *interrogate*," said Simon.

"Shut up!" Ruthie cried. "I'm the law around here."

Simon surrendered as Ruthie wrapped the rope around his body again and again.

"Aren't you bored yet?" he asked his little sister.

"No way!" Ruthie declared. "I have to book you next. And then we'll have a trial."

Great, Simon thought as Ruthie finished tying him up. *Just what I wanted out of my first baby-sitting experience. To go to jail.*

"Matt, we were just talking, I promise. Nothing—"

But Matt's stare cut Jordan's explanation short.

"I don't want to talk to you, Jordan," Matt said angrily. "Not yet, anyway." Matt shot a hard look at his sister. "Lucc!" he barked again.

Mortified, Lucy climbed out of Jordan's car. She walked to Matt's Camaro with her head down.

Jordan climbed out of his car, too. He walked around the Camaro and opened the door for Lucy. She got into the back seat, refusing to look at her brother. Jordan bent down and peered into Matt's window. "We *were* just talking," he said to Matt again.

"Fine," Matt said, still not looking at him. "Now Lucy and I are going to talk, too. Good night."

"Could you wait to talk to your dad?"

Jordan asked. "I'd like to speak with him first."

"That's not a good idea," Lucy yelled from her side of the car.

"Look," Matt said, facing Jordan at last. "You do whatever you think is right. But I think what's best for you right now is to get into your car."

Jordan stepped back and held up his hands. "I'm going," he said. He glared at Lucy. "I'll talk to you later." Then Jordan climbed into his car and sat behind the wheel.

Matt turned to Lucy, who now was staring at him. A thousand emotions danced across her face. Matt thought she was about to cry. But Lucy surprised him. She began to pound him with her fists as hard as she could.

"Who do you think you are, embarrassing me like that?" Lucy howled. "I'm not a child. I'm practically a grown woman, and you have no right to interfere with my life like this!"

Matt sat and took Lucy's pounding until her rage was nearly spent. Then he reached out held her hands.

"I'm sorry," Matt said, his voice softer. "But I'd rather embarrass you than find out later that you did something really stupid."

"Oh, yeah!" Lucy cried. "Well, if you want to find one of your sisters doing something stupid, why don't you burst in on Mary at her little boy-girl sleepover!"

Matt looked at Lucy, stunned. Lucy turned and looked at Jordan. He frowned, waved to her, and drove away.

Matt threw the Camaro into gear.

"Where are you going," Lucy asked urgently.

"To the Caldwells," Matt said through clenched teeth.

Mary and Frank Malone had stayed in the walk-in closet for most of the evening. They had finished all the cookies, talked each other's ears off getting to know one another, and were now growing sleepy. Mary was just dozing off when she heard a commotion outside the door.

She opened her eyes. Frank was looking at her.

"What's going on?" Mary asked groggily.

Frank looked sick. "Out there," he said, pointing. "Some crazy guy's doing a lot of yelling. I think it's your brother."

"Mary!" Matt hollered. "Where are you!"

"He sounds—"

"Really mad," Frank said, finishing her thought.

Mary rose and opened the closet door.

Matt was standing in the middle of the Caldwells' living room. Half the varsity team was there with him. They were all trying to keep out of his way.

"Mary!" Matt cried.

"Did Lucy rat on me?" Mary immediately demanded.

Matt ignored the question. His eyes went wide when Mary swung the closet door all the way open and he saw Frank Malone standing behind her and the sleeping bag spread out on the closet floor.

"Get your stuff!" Matt cried. "We're going home."

"But we weren't doing anything wrong!" Mary said.

"*Now,* Mary!" Matt barked.

Mary looked behind her and realized what it must look like to Matt. Her eyes met Frank's and he frowned.

It's all about perception versus reality, Mary thought bitterly as she packed up her stuff.

NINE

Simon struggled against the rope, but it was hopeless—Ruthie had tied him up nice and tight. He looked up and saw Ruthie sitting on the staircase, a few steps above him. She was eating a cookie.

"Untie me," Simon said. "Just untie me, okay?"

"I can't," Ruthie explained between bites. "I'm only the bank teller. You have to wait until the detectives come and irrigate you."

"*Interrogate!*" Simon said, losing his patience.

"Yeah," Ruthie said, picking a crumb off her shirt. "That."

Simon rolled his eyes. "Well, pretend to

be the detective now," he insisted. "You don't want Mom and Dad to come home and find me like this, do you?"

Simon immediately knew it was a stupid question. *Of course she does!*

"I don't know," Ruthie said. "You look pretty cute like that. Let me see you from another angle."

Now Simon was seething. But he was completely helpless—Ruthie had skillfully roped him in while he wasn't paying attention. She got up and brushed the cookie crumbs off her clothes. Then she climbed two steps, stuck her head between the stair rails, and took a long look at her brother.

"Yep!" she said. "You look cute from here, too. Like you're behind bars."

"This isn't funny, Ruthie!"

"Oh, yes it is," she said, laughing. But when she started to pull her head out from between the rails, it got stuck. She tugged again and her ears began to hurt. Ruthie started screaming.

"Don't panic!" Simon cried, a fair amount of panic in *his* voice, too.

"I can't get my head out!" Ruthie howled. "This is all *your* fault."

Just then, Happy waddled into the foyer, carrying her food bowl in her mouth.

She dropped it at Simon's feet and whimpered.

"Listen to me, girl," Simon said. "Chew the ropes. Chew the ropes, girl!"

Happy wagged her tail uncertainly. Then she yawned, stretched out on the floor, and turned her belly up to Simon.

"Stupid dog," Simon muttered.

"You're the worst baby-sitter I've ever had," Ruthie said.

Simon frowned. "That's not what you said two hours ago."

"That was before you made me become part of the staircase!" Ruthie struggled to get her head out, but she was still trapped. "I hope Dad has a chainsaw," she said.

They heard a car pull into the driveway.

Please be Matt, please be Matt, Simon thought nervously.

The Reverend and Mrs. Camden were quiet on their ride home. They had dropped Cassandra and Barbara off with their parents. The girls' problems with their boyfriends had not been resolved, and they probably wouldn't be for many years—if ever.

"We're so lucky," Mrs. Camden said, thinking about their own children.

"I know," Rev. Camden said, nodding. "Matt is mature and responsible—most of the time."

"And he's great at keeping an eye on the others," Mrs. Camden added.

"And both Mary and Lucy have good heads on their shoulders," Rev. Camden continued.

They drove on in silence for a while.

"I'm glad that Mary, Lucy, and Ruthie will never have to go through what Barbara and Cassandra are experiencing," Mrs. Camden said.

They turned the corner and pulled into the driveway. Rev. Camden cut the engine and got out. He circled the car to open the door for his wife.

"And I'm so proud of Simon, too," Mrs. Camden continued. "He's doing his best to take care of Ruthie," she said.

"And I'm sure he did a great job," Rev. Camden said as they walked up to the front door. "I think we can really trust Simon."

Rev. Camden opened the front door, and Mrs. Camden gasped when she saw Simon tied up and Ruthie with her head stuck in the staircase.

"Hi, Mommy," Ruthie said.

"She—she didn't want to play board

games," Simon stammered.

Mrs. Camden ran to free Ruthie. Simon looked mighty embarrassed. Rev. and Mrs. Camden exchanged meaningful glances as they set to work.

"Looks like we may have been wrong about Simon's baby-sitting abilities," Mrs. Camden said.

Rev. Camden nodded. "I hope that's not all we're wrong about."

Lucy watched from the back seat as Matt escorted Mary down the Caldwells' walk. Neither of them was talking—Mary looked upset and Matt looked angry.

"Get in," Matt barked, opening the car door for Mary. As Mary climbed into the passenger seat, she shot a hard look at Lucy.

"After this sentence, I'm not speaking to you for the rest of your life," Mary said to Lucy.

"Oh, yes you are," Matt said sternly as he climbed behind the wheel. "And you're both going to speak to me," he lectured. "And I'm going to speak to the two of you, too."

"Well," Lucy said, her voice tight with emotion. "Can we not speak to Mom and

Dad and just keep this among the three of us?"

Mary and Lucy both gazed at Matt hopefully. He gripped the steering wheel and thought about it, refusing to look at his sisters.

Frank Malone arrived at the Camden house just as Jordan was parking his car. The two boys got out of their vehicles and walked toward each other. No words were spoken, but they exchanged meaningful looks.

"Was your date cut short, too?" Jordan finally asked.

Frank nodded. "Sort of."

"Looks like we both hit some rough weather," Jordan observed.

"Yeah," Frank replied. "Hurricane Matt…"

Together, the two boys walked up the sidewalk and rang the Camdens' doorbell.

Fifteen minutes later, Rev. Camden and his wife knew the whole story. They didn't like what they heard, but both of them realized that things could have been much, much worse.

"So that's when Matt pulled up and told

Lucy to get in the car with him," Jordan explained, his eyes on the carpet. "I let her go because I thought I knew a confrontation wasn't the way to go. But nothing was going to happen between Lucy and me."

Jordan looked up. Rev. and Mrs. Camden sat on the couch, opposite the two boys. For a long time, they said nothing.

"Any idea where Matt and Lucy are now?" Rev. Camden asked finally.

Jordan shrugged. "I think they're on their way back from the Caldwells'," he said.

Frank nodded. "Sounds right to me," he agreed.

"So Matt didn't know that the basketball sleepover was co-ed," said Mrs. Camden.

Both boys nodded. "I guess you guys didn't know either," Jordan said.

Mrs. Camden shook her head, trying not to get upset. "Why did she lie to us?" she said.

"She didn't think she was lying," answered Jordan. "She just thought she was fudging the truth by not mentioning that boys would be there, too."

"It amounts to the same thing, Jordan," Rev. Camden said, his anger showing. Then he paused and smiled at the two boys. "But we shouldn't blame either of you," he said.

Jordan and Frank sighed in relief.

"You were both very brave to come forward like this," Rev. Camden continued. "I respect you for it."

Mrs. Camden nodded. "I agree," she said. "You've done your parents proud."

"I didn't do it to impress my folks," Frank said. "I came to you because it was the right thing to do."

"And I believe that you wouldn't be talking to us unless you were telling the truth," Rev. Camden said.

Again, the boys nodded.

Rev. Camden sighed. "Let me tell you some truths," the Reverend said in a very serious tone. "You are both mature, and I honor what you did tonight." Rev. Camden turned to Jordan. "In your case, you're two years older than my daughter. You're a senior and a handsome young man, so it's more than likely that you've already had some...experience."

Jordan blushed but said nothing.

"So here's the deal," Rev. Camden continued. "You are not to be alone with my daughter again outside of this house.

Group activities, school functions—that's it."

Jordan nodded.

Then Rev. Camden turned to Frank. "We've know each other a very short time," he began. "But you shouldn't have been alone with Mary at a co-ed sleepover."

Frank sighed. Then he nodded in agreement.

"But at least you came forward," Rev. Camden added, softening the blow. He leaned back and looked at the teenagers. "I want both of you to come over to the house more often."

Frank and Jordan stared at Rev. Camden, surprised at his offer.

"I agree," Mrs. Camden said. "I want to get to know both of you better, and to spend some time with you. You should feel free to bring your parents by to meet us, too."

Frank looked a little alarmed.

"It doesn't have to be anything formal," Mrs. Camden continued. "Just drop by with one or the other or both if you like."

"And I want us to keep talking," Rev. Camden said. "Just like we've done tonight. I want you both to know that despite what I heard about this particular evening, I think you're responsible, honest guys who respect my daughters." Rev. Camden paused. "And I like that," he said finally. "I really do."

"And so do I," Mrs. Camden agreed.

"As much as I hate to break this up," Rev. Camden said, "I don't think you boys want to be here when the girls get home with Matt."

Frank and Jordan both nodded.

They rose.

"Thanks a lot, Rev. and Mrs. Camden. "I'm going to head home," Jordan said. "I guess I'll see you in church on Sunday."

As Rev. and Mrs. Camden escorted the young men to the front door, it swung open and Matt, Mary, and Lucy came in.

The girls froze when they saw their dates and the looks of anger and disappointment on their parents' faces.

"I'll call you tomorrow, Lucy," Jordan said, rushing past her to his car.

"I hope I can see you again," Frank said to Mary before he ducked out the door.

Matt looked at his parents. "I've already talked to them," he said.

"Thank you, Matt. Good-night," Rev. Camden said.

Matt patted his sisters on the back and

gave them a sympathetic look. He ran upstairs.

"Mary," Mrs. Camden said. "I'd like to talk to you in the kitchen." Then she looked at Lucy. "And I'll have a word with you after you talk to your father."

Lucy nodded sadly.

Just then, Matt came bounding downstairs, clutching his video camera.

"Wait a minute!" he cried. "Would anyone mind if I taped this?"

The camera work was shaky, and some of the angles were all wrong. But the visual presentation had power and rang true.

The footage began in the Camdens' kitchen. First, the camera pointed at the clock on the wall. The time was 1:34 A.M. Then the camera panned to Mrs. Camden and Mary. They sat together at the kitchen table. Mrs. Camden looked upset; Mary looked uncomfortable.

"But I wasn't going to have sex," Mary maintained. "And even if I were, I wouldn't have to go to a basketball sleepover to do it."

Mrs. Camden blinked in surprise as she thought about Mary's troubling words. Finally, she sighed. "Good point," she said.

Mary sat back in her chair and smiled.

"Okay," Mrs. Camden said after a pause. "Then under what circumstances would you consider having sex?"

It was Mary's turn to be surprised. Instead of answering her mother, Mary looked right into the camera, completely embarrassed.

As the second scene in Matt's video began, the clock on the kitchen wall read 2:13 A.M. Mary was still at the table, but Mrs. Camden had been replaced by the Reverend. He looked at Mary, who avoided his gaze.

"We keep coming back to the question of why you'd lie about it if there was nothing wrong with what you were doing," he said.

"Because *you* think there's something wrong with what I was doing," Mary cried. "But I don't think it was wrong. I just don't."

Rev. Camden nodded.

"Okay," he said, holding up his hand. "But still, if you feel mature enough to make your own decisions, then why aren't you mature enough to stand up for those same decisions instead of trying to sneak around behind our backs?"

Mary thought about it for a moment. Then she looked up into the camera lens, her face gripped by emotion.

For the third scene, the action moved from the kitchen to the living room couch. The camera panned around the room until it focused on the clock on the mantle. The time was three A.M. Lucy sat next to her mother. The discussion was heated.

"I don't know," Lucy argued. "I'm not sure I even know what the options are."

"But it's important to have a plan," Mrs. Camden said. "And the plan I'd like you to have is to wait until you're married to have sex."

"Okay," Lucy said. "But isn't there something in between those extremes?"

"Extremes?" Mrs. Camden said, confused.

Lucy nodded. "You know," she continued. "More than just kissing, but less than going all the way?" She stared at her mother. "Where do you draw the line?" she asked.

This time, it was Mrs. Camden who stared at the camera, completely embarrassed.

*   *   *

The final scene in the video presentation was quiet. The camera panned around the living room once more before focusing on the clock. It was six A.M.

Mary was asleep on a chair, where she had passed out hours before. Lucy was stretched out on the floor with a comforter over her. Rev. Camden and Mrs. Camden sat on the couch, also asleep.

As they dozed, the camera moved to the foyer, where Ruthie and Simon were coming down the stairs. The kids were still in their pajamas.

"Why not?" Ruthie said.

"No!" Simon replied. "I'm giving up on this baby-sitting gig."

"But why?" Ruthie whined.

"Because kids shouldn't be taking care of kids," Simon declared. "I'm too young."

Simon walked through the living room and headed for the kitchen. The camera stayed on Ruthie as she crawled up onto her parents' laps. Rev. Camden and Mrs. Camden stirred and opened their eyes. They didn't notice that the camera was still on them.

"Mommy," Ruthie began. "I have a question."

"Shoot," Mrs. Camden said, stretching.

"Where do babies come from?"

Rev. Camden and Mrs. Camden exchanged looks. Then they pulled Ruthie into their arms and hugged her.

The picture on the television screen turned to snow. Matt flicked a button on the remote, and the television went black. Mary and Lucy, who were sitting next to each other on the couch, turned as one to their older brother.

"How come you didn't put in the answers?" Lucy asked.

Matt smiled. "Because not everyone would answer the questions in the same way," he explained.

Mary nodded. "So," she asked, "what are you going to call it?"

"I thought about calling it 'Let's Talk About Sex,'" Matt said. "But I just thought of a better title."

"And that is?" Lucy asked.

"'The Talk,'" Matt said. "'The Nineteen-Year Talk.'"

Without another word, Matt popped the tape out of the VCR and left the room. Mary and Lucy watched their older brother run up the stairs.

"You know," Mary said, "there are a few things I'd like to ask *him*."

Lucy smiled. "Me too!"

"Hey, Matt!" the girls shouted, running up the stairs after him.

TEN

The crazy weekend became just a memory as Monday arrived. Lucy found Jordan in the halls and apologized for McArthur's Point. He laughed and told her that it would have been fun, *if* they had been older and much wiser than they were right now.

Frank found Mary and apologized for going to her parents. To his surprise, Mary wasn't upset. They agreed to see each other later in the week—at a school function, of course. Mary realized she was starting to like Frank a lot.

At three o'clock, the school bell rang. Mary and Lucy met at the front door and headed for the street. Their mother was waiting for them in the station wagon.

"You can drive," Mrs. Camden said to Mary. She slid over to the passenger side, and Mary climbed in behind the wheel. Lucy hopped into the back seat, waving to some of her friends.

Mary threw the car into drive and was about to pull away when her mother stopped her. "I forgot," Mrs. Camden said. "One of the reasons I came to pick you up was because I wanted to thank your driver's ed teacher."

Mary quickly put the car in park. "What—what for?" She stammered, panic rising.

"For helping you get your license, silly," Mrs. Camden said. "So let's go over there!" she said, pointing. "Just park over there so I can get out."

Mary looked where her mother was pointing. Her panic increased.

"I could thank him *for* you," Mary suggested. She heard Lucy snickering in the back seat.

"No, no!" Mrs. Camden said. "That's not polite."

"Why not?" Mary asked.

Mrs. Camden ignored her daughter. "Just pull in between those two cars," she said, still pointing. "Right over there."

Mary looked in the rearview mirror. She could see that Lucy was enjoying this.

"But that's...that's the principal's car," Mary said.

"And you think the principal minds if someone parks behind her car?" Mrs. Camden said. The look in her mother's eye told Mary that her number was up. But she decided to pull the car up alongside the principal's and make an attempt to parallel park anyway.

"I think I'll just get out here," Lucy said nervously as Mary began the maneuver.

"Stay put," Mrs. Camden said. "This will only take a minute."

Mary threw the car into reverse and tried to park. But after repeated attempts—and lots of jostling—she failed miserably. Her bad driving had actually attracted a crowd. Even the principal had arrived and was watching.

Mary sighed and threw the car into park, even though it was still sitting in the middle of the road.

"That's what I thought," Mrs. Camden said finally. "I asked you the other day if the test examiner made you parallel park, and you said yes."

"Well, he did," Mary said.

"And?"

Mary sighed, deciding to give up. "And I cried so he would let me out of it," she confessed.

Mrs. Camden turned to the back seat and looked at Lucy. "Why do I think *you* had something to do with this?"

Lucy stopped snickering.

"Because I...did?" she said sheepishly.

Mrs. Camden rolled her eyes. "Do you know what the problem in our family really is?" she asked.

Mary and Lucy both shook their heads.

"It's that my daughters are such terrible liars."

"Huh?"

Mrs. Camden smiled. "It's not that you lie, because you don't. Well, not very often anyway," she said. "It's that you do it so badly. You're both amateurs, thank goodness."

Then Mrs. Camden shot Lucy a look. "You!" she said. "No more crying to get your way."

Lucy opened her mouth to protest, but thought better of it and just nodded.

Then Mrs. Camden looked at Mary. "And you! I'm driving," she said, pushing her oldest daughter out the driver's side door. "And you're going to practice a lot more before you re-take that driver's test."

Mary sighed. "Okay, Okay. But will you just get this car as far as possible away from the principal? *Please?*"

WIN A TRIP TO HOLLYWOOD!

Official Rules & Regulations

I. HOW TO ENTER

NO PURCHASE NECESSARY. Enter by printing your full name, address, phone number, date of birth, and answer to "What character gets kissed by a stranger?" on a piece of paper, and mailing it to "*7th Heaven* Win a Trip to Hollywood!" Sweepstakes, Random House Children's Books Marketing Department, 1540 Broadway, 19th Floor, New York, NY 10036. Entries must be mailed separately and received by Random House no later than July 31, 2001. LIMIT ONE ENTRY PER PERSON. Partially completed or illegible entries will not be accepted. Sponsors are not responsible for lost, late, mutilated, illegible, stolen, postage-due, incomplete, or misdirected entries. All entries become the property of Random House and will not be returned, so please keep a copy for your records.

II. ELIGIBILITY

Sweepstakes is open to legal residents of the United States, excluding the state of Arizona and Puerto Rico, who are between the ages of 9 and 16 as of July 31, 2001. All federal, state, and local laws and regulations apply. Void wherever prohibited or restricted by law. Employees of Random House Inc., Paramount, Viacom Company, Spelling Television Inc., and their parent companies, assigns, subsidiaries, or affiliates; advertising, promotion, and fulfillment agencies; and their immediate families and persons living in their household are not eligible to enter this sweepstakes.

III. PRIZE

One Grand Prize Winner will win a trip to Hollywood and a Paramount lot tour to the set of *7th Heaven*, including airfare, ground transportation to and from set, lot tour, and airport, a hotel stay for two nights for the winner and one parent/legal guardian, autographed photos of the *7th Heaven* cast, guided lot tour for winner and one parent/legal guardian, and lunch in executive dining room for winner and one parent/legal guardian. (Approximate retail value $1,500.00 U.S.) No other expenses included. Travel and use of accommodations are at risk of winner and winner's parent/legal guardian, and Random House Inc., Paramount, Viacom Company, and Spelling Television Inc. do not assume any liability. If for any reason prize is not available or cannot be fulfilled, Random House Inc. reserves the right to substitute a prize of equal or greater value, including—but not limited to—cash equivalent, which is at the complete discretion of Random House Inc. Taxes, if any, are the winner's sole responsibility. Prizes are not transferable and cannot be assigned. No prize or cash substitutes allowed, except at the discretion of the sponsor as set forth above.

IV. WINNER

Odds of winning depend on total number of entries received. One winner will be selected in a random drawing on or about August 15, 2001, from all eligible entries with the correct answer received within the entry deadline by the Random House Children's Books Marketing Department. By participating, entrants agree to be bound by the official rules and the decision of the judges, which shall be final and binding in all respects. The Grand Prize Winner will win a trip to Hollywood and the set of *7th Heaven*. The prize will be awarded in the name of the winner's parent or legal guardian. Winner's parent or legal guardian will be notified by mail and winner's parent/legal guardian will be required to sign and return affidavit(s) of eligibility and release of liability within 14 days of notification. A noncompliance within that time period or the return of any notification as undeliverable will result in disqualification and the selection of an alternate winner. In the event of any other noncompliance with rules and conditions, prize may be awarded to an alternate winner. Other entry names will NOT be used for subsequent mail solicitation.

V. RESERVATIONS

By participating, winner (and winner's parent/legal guardian) agrees that Random House, Paramount, Viacom Company, Spelling Television Inc., their parent companies, assigns, subsidiaries, or affiliates and advertising, promotion, and fulfillment agencies will have no liability whatsoever and will be held harmless by winner (and winner's parent/legal guardian) for any liability for any injuries, losses, or damages of any kind to person, including death, and property, resulting in whole or in part, directly or indirectly, from the acceptance, possession, misuse, or use of the prize, or participation in this sweepstakes. By entering the sweepstakes winner's parent or legal guardian consents to the use of the winner's name, likeness, and biographical data for publicity and promotional purposes on behalf of Random House, Paramount, Viacom Company, and Spelling Television Inc., with no additional compensation or further permission (except where prohibited by law). Other entry names will NOT be used for subsequent mail solicitation. For the name of the winner, available after August 15, 2001, please send a stamped, self-addressed envelope to: Random House Children's Books Marketing Department, "*7th Heaven* Win a Trip to Hollywood!" Sweepstakes Winner, 1540 Broadway, 19th Floor, New York, NY 10036. Washington and Vermont residents may omit return postage.

7th Heaven™

WIN A TRIP TO HOLLYWOOD!

Visit the set of *7th Heaven* and receive VIP treatment at Paramount Pictures. Watch the *7th Heaven* show on the WB network during the month of May to answer the following question correctly and you'll automatically be entered in a drawing to win a trip to Hollywood and the set of *7th Heaven*.

Question: What character gets kissed by a stranger?

See opposite page for official sweepstakes rules.

RANDOM HOUSE
CHILDREN'S BOOKS

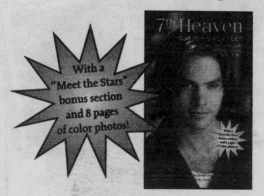

MARY'S STORY

Big sis Mary seems to have it all together: She's practical, super-smart, beautiful, vivacious, and a rising star on her school's basketball team. But beneath her perfect exterior, sixteen-year-old Mary is struggling to figure out boys, friends, parents, and life in general—not to mention her younger sister Lucy!

MATT'S
STORY

As the oldest kid in the Camden clan and a college freshman, handsome eighteen-year-old Matt
often bears the burden of playing referee
between his siblings and his parents. Sometimes
it's tough to balance family loyalty against a
fierce desire for independence, but Matt has
earned his reputation as the "responsible one"—
most of the time.